A Husband for Melanie

Oakdale Romance Duet

CHERYL WRIGHT

Contents:

Acknowledgements

Thanks to my very dear friends (and authors), Margaret Tanner and Susan Horsnell.

Without their encouragement and help, I would never have embarked on this amazing journey.

I also want to say thanks to Susan for the amazing covers she always manages to create for me.

To Alan, my husband of over 44 years, thanks for being a relentless supporter of my writing for more years than I care to remember.

About the Author

Multi-published, best selling and award-winning author, Cheryl Wright, former secretary, debt collector, account manager, writing coach, and shopping tour hostess, loves reading.

She writes both contemporary and historical western romance, as well as contemporary romance and romantic suspense.

She lives in Melbourne, Australia, and is married with two adult children and has six grandchildren.

When she's not writing, she can be found in her craft room making greeting cards.

Check out Cheryl's Amazon page - https://www.amazon.com/author/cherylwright for a full list of her other books.

Other Links:

http://cheryl-wright.com

https://www.facebook.com/cherylwrightauthor

Newsletter

http://cheryl-wright.com/newsletter.html

Chapter One

Melanie Chalmers sat with the telephone to her ear.

"Of course, Mr Gregson." She paused for a moment to let him continue speaking. "I totally understand, but you need to understand the bank's position on this."

Charles Gregson continued his angry tirade for some minutes, but thankfully disconnected the call a short time later.

Melanie sat at her desk with her hands to her face; she'd taken more calls like this one in the past six months than she had in the past few years. Tightening of the rules had led to this abhorrent situation.

Being Loans Manager at the bank was not only stressful, it was downright detrimental to her health. Something had to change.

The phone ringing again startled her. She stared down at it for long moments before reluctantly picking it up.

"Loans Office. Melanie speaking." Her heart beat loud in her chest, waiting for the next round of abuse.

"Mel, it's Sierra."

Melanie let go of the breath she'd been holding. "Oh thank goodness it's you. I..." She couldn't continue, she was feeling so emotional after the nasty call she'd just dealt with.

"Are you alright, Mel?" She could tell Sierra anything. They'd known each other for most of their lives and been best friends at school.

"Not really." Her voice was breaking. She needed to pull herself together - fast.

"I'm sorry, Mel. Take a deep breath, then breathe out slowly." She waited while Mel did as she'd said before continuing. "Better?"

"A little," Mel said. "Thanks. I needed that."

"Good. Let's talk about it tonight. I was ringing to see if you'd like to come for dinner." Sierra sounded genuinely concerned, and Melanie knew she would be. But Sierra knew she couldn't talk when she was at work. Apart from her heavy workload, there were too many prying ears around.

Melanie heard the baby crying in the background. "Sounds like Cody wants you," she said, with more cheer in her heart at the mere thought of her little cousin.

"So you'll come?"

"Absolutely. I wouldn't miss it for the world."

* * *

"**A**nd basically, that's what happened. Not that it's anything new – different day, different client, same story."

Sierra reached out and patted her hand at the same time breast-feeding two-month-old Cody. Her husband Braxton, Melanie's cousin, eye-balled his wife.

"Well, that's one of the reasons we invited you tonight." Sierra glanced across to Braxton who was sitting on the edge of his seat.

"I'm far from ready to go back to working at the inn, and to be honest, I'm not sure I ever will be."

Mel was rocked by the news.

Sierra owned the recently restored Oakdale Inn, where the pair were married a little over a year ago. She loved the inn, but Melanie knew she loved Cody even more, so she really shouldn't be surprised.

"I'll still be around, but nowhere near as much," she added. "My family is my priority now."

"We know how stressed you've been at the bank these past months," Braxton added. "And thought this would be ideal for you."

"We're offering it to you before anyone else," Sierra added.

Melanie's heart rate accelerated. Could it be true? They were offering her a job? Working at the Oakdale Inn would be a dream job for her.

She clapped her hands together. "Yes! I'll take the job!" She wriggled around in her seat, barely able to control her excitement.

Sierra grinned at her husband. "Hang on," she said, gazing at Melanie. "You don't know what the job is yet. I could be offering you anything."

But Mel knew that wouldn't be the case. Sierra was always very careful about matching her employees to the right position.

Suddenly she felt deflated. "Oh. But I have to give notice to the bank."

"We know. We're willing to wait." Sierra put Cody to her shoulder and gently patted his back.

Braxton leaned forward. "It will be much less stress, but you will need to work some weekends. Will that work for you?"

She didn't have to think twice. "Absolutely. I don't have a social life anyway."

"Don't you want to know what we're offering? You're not even slightly interested?" Braxton chuckled.

Mel and Braxton were very close. She knew she could trust him.

She grinned. "Okay, go on then – tell me."

"You will be our Guest Services Manager."

Mel didn't even know what that was.

"You will interact with the guests and ensure their stay is above their expectations." Sierra explained.

"Ah, I'm not sure what that entails." She frowned and was more confused that ever. How did one do that?

"It's a lot of little things. You'll oversee the Concierge and Valet services, ensure the guests are happy, deal with complaints should there being any, which hopefully there aren't. So many things – organize day tours when needed, I could go on and on."

Mel was relieved. "So basically, I just keep the guests happy?"

"That's it."

"Okay, I accept." She couldn't stop grinning. This job would be a welcome change of pace.

She mentally did the arithmetic in her head. "After I give notice at the bank, I could start, say, mid-April?"

"Make it May 1. That way you get a break before you start. Sound good?"

"Sounds great."

The conversation turned to salary, uniforms, and expectations. Melanie knew she'd be leaving her soul-destroying job and that was all that mattered to her.

She knew no matter what, Brax and Sierra would look after her and treat her fairly.

The weight that had held her down for a long time had suddenly lifted and she felt like a totally different person. Tomorrow she would give her notice, and her life would be changed forever.

Only one other thing would make her life better, and that would be a cuddle with dear little Cody before he was tucked into bed.

* * *

"But you can't leave, Melanie. We rely on you. *I* rely on you – you're the best Loans Manager I've ever had." Her boss was far from happy.

"I'm sorry, Mr Howard," she said. "But this has been coming for a long time. The changes the bank made to the loans process has left the staff open for abuse."

He looked shaken but said nothing.

"Every day, at least once an hour, we cop abuse from disgruntled customers. I can't take it any more." She sighed. "Besides, my cousin and his wife have offered me a dream job at the Oakdale Inn."

He sat there behind his huge mahogany desk, with his gold-plated name and his fancy telephone. His lips were pursed, and he was glaring at her, but still said nothing. It was then realization hit. He knew! He was fully aware of the verbal abuse staff were enduring but had done nothing. He just didn't care.

Fury boiled up inside her, making her resolve stronger than ever.

She handed over her resignation paperwork, almost threw it at him, and left the bank manager's office without another word. He was far from happy, and neither was Mel.

If he'd thought about the repercussions on the staff before making any changes, this wouldn't be happening.

She took deep breaths, willing herself to calm down. She only had another two weeks here – she needed to keep that in mind.

When she had calmed down enough, she made a cup of tea, then proceeded to her desk. The desk she'd sat at for the past nine years. This had been her first job out of school. Braxton had tried to talk her out of it, but she wouldn't listen.

"Come and work for me," he'd said, but she didn't want to work on his property. She wanted a real job – one that she found herself and had no connection to family.

It had been the perfect job in the beginning, but after her promotion, and the changes to the bank's loans rules, it had all gone to hell.

She closed her eyes and shrugged her shoulders until she was more relaxed.

If she had felt the weight lift last night, then right now she was floating on air. The headache that had been hanging around for months finally lifted, and her whole demeanor felt different, better.

She was joyful. She hadn't felt that way for as long as she could remember, and she knew with her new job, it would continue. She couldn't wait for May to roll around.

* * *

Saying goodbye to the colleagues she'd worked with for nearly a decade had been difficult.

The bank had put on an afternoon tea for her, and speeches were made. Mr Howard stated how sad he was to see her go, then everyone tucked into the abundance of food on the surrounding tables.

Melanie cleared her desk of all her personal items, which were very few, slung her bag over her shoulder, and headed for the elevator.

After all this time, it was hard to believe she would never return. Someone else would sit at her little desk; the one she'd sat at all this time.

It was all she could do not to cry.

"Mel." She turned to see Sharon Stanton standing nearby. "I'm really going to miss you," she said, wrapping her arms around her friend. "But I know this is the best thing for you."

"Thanks Sharon," she said quietly, trying not to break down. She'd hoped to sneak out before actual goodbye's had to happen. "I'll probably see you around town."

They separated, and Melanie slowly walked away, her heart hammering in her chest. She knew she'd done the right thing. She could not have continued working at the bank under such horrendous conditions. Her mental health was in grave danger and had been for some time.

She pressed the button to the elevator and waited for it to arrive. All the while, Sharon stood staring after her, looking deflated.

If it wasn't for the anticipation of starting a new and exciting job, she would probably feel the same.

She exited the elevator and slowly walked toward the front door, where she would leave for the very last time.

Melanie looked around. "Goodbye bank," she said under her breath, then walked out the door, determined not to look back.

Chapter Two

Mel took a deep breath, then walked through the door to the Oakdale Inn.

Her two-week break had done her the world of good. Brax and Sierra were right to insist she wait until now to start her new job.

She was refreshed and ready to move forward.

She'd been here before, but not as an employee. The last time she'd been at the inn was the day of the wedding. Sierra and Braxton's wedding. It was all hustle and not a lot of time to look around. Apart from the fact it was still under construction – almost finished but not quite there yet.

This would be a whole different ball game.

She glanced down at her uniform, which was basically a suit with the Oakdale Inn logo, and ensured it looked as it should. She tugged at her skirt to straighten out a few wrinkles that were showing.

Cassie Somerton was the manager of the inn and greeted her at the door. "Welcome, welcome!" she said, with a smile on her face.

"Thank you," Mel said, relieved to see a familiar face.

"I'll give you the grand tour, beginning with the staff amenities." She led Mel to a backroom used solely for staff lockers. "This is your locker," she said. "And here are your keys. Please ensure you use them." She also handed Mel a lanyard with her staff identification.

She pointed to another room which lead off the locker room. "Change rooms are over there, and this is the staff break room," she said, walking into yet another room. "We look after our staff very well here, as you will see." She indicated the kettle, a microwave, toaster and more. "The fridge is *always* filled with food. Just help yourself."

"When you come on shift, fill out one of these forms," she said, indicating a bundle of forms on a clip-board. "Philippe Bisset, our head chef, will provide whichever meal you choose while you are on a shift."

"Seriously?" Mel couldn't believe it.

"Like I said, we look after our staff." She turned to face Melanie. "I don't know how to say this any other way, so I'm just going to come out with it." She took a deep breath, as if bracing herself. "There will be no special consideration because you are part of Sierra's family. No offense intended."

"None taken. Look, I don't expect special treatment. I hope it wasn't suggested because…"

"No. Definitely not." Cassie was quick to reassure her. "We'll continue our tour, and then we'll talk about your job description."

Mel was in awe. The day of the wedding, she'd not seen all the rooms and facilities available, and not all rooms were complete. A lot had been done since she was last here.

"And this is our beautifully equipped kitchen." She turned to the head chef. "Philippe, I'd like to introduce you to our newest staff member, Melanie Chalmers."

"Chalmers, as in Sierra and Braxton?" He asked in his enchanting French accent. His hand was outstretched, and Melanie accepted it. It was soft and warm, and his grip gentle. Mel was certain his demeanor would be the same.

A zing went up her arm as their hands connected.

"Brax is my cousin," she said. "Please, treat me like every other staff member. I'll be very upset if you don't."

"I can see we're going to get along just fine."

She glanced around the kitchen. "This is massive."

"It is. Sierra installed a brand-new kitchen with the renovations. Here," he said, putting a hand to her back. "Come and meet my sous-chef and kitchen hands."

She was introduced to everyone, then the two women headed for Cassie's office.

"Philippe is nice," she said conversationally.

"Yeah, he is." She unlocked the door to her office, indicating for Mel to sit, and they discussed her position and all it entailed.

Mel immediately felt right at home here and had no regrets about leaving her old job behind.

* * *

"Aren't you going home, Mel?" Cassie pulled on her jacket and headed for the door. "It's been a long day for you. So much to take in."

"Thanks, but I have a few more things I want to check out before I go." She sat behind the front desk, checking the guest list for tomorrow.

Cassie had forewarned her there were some high-profile guests arriving over the next few days, and she wanted to be prepared.

"Okay. I'll see you tomorrow then." She waved and left, leaving Mel to check the upcoming bookings.

"Ah, Melanie, are you free?" Philippe's alluring accent flooded her ears.

She glanced up. "I'll be leaving in an hour or so, but I'm free right now."

His arm outstretched, he reached for her hand. "Allow me."

He led her to the inn's restaurant, which was currently empty. "Please sit. I shall return shortly." He left her to wonder what on earth he was up to.

Melanie glanced up as he returned to the room. "It will get crazy here very soon, so I like to take a short break before it does. I thought you might also enjoy a break."

He took two coffees and a small plate of sweet pastries from a tray and placed them on the table.

"That looks amazing. Thank you for thinking of me."

He shrugged. "It is purely selfish. I want to get to know you better. We will be working together after all."

She smiled. She'd only met him this morning, but Mel already felt as though she'd known Philippe for years.

She took a sip of her coffee. "Perfect."

He lifted the plate and offered her a mini chocolate éclair. "Please," he said. "Made with my own two hands. Especially for you."

She felt the heat creep up her face. "I doubt it," she said with a laugh.

He was gallant enough to look guilty. "Okay, perhaps not just for you. But I made them with you in mind."

She reached over and took one, snatching up a napkin as she did. "Oh my. These are delicious," she said, genuinely meaning it. "Did you really make these?"

"I should be offended," he said, grinning. "Do you think I am not capable? My dear lady, this is child's play. Next time I shall make something much more to your liking."

His eyes sparkled playfully, and she admitted defeat. "No one has ever gone to such trouble for me before," she said, then took another bite. "These really are to die for."

"My éclairs will not kill you, Madame," he said playfully.

Melanie was really enjoying the interaction with Philippe and couldn't wait for next time.

* * *

Melanie flopped into bed, more exhausted than she'd been in a long time.

But it was good exhaustion. Not stress-related, and not from being verbally abused. Her new work colleagues were all lovely. Especially Philippe.

She realized after she'd left work they'd met before. Very briefly at the wedding.

He must think her terrible, to not remember having met him. They hadn't spoke, but he'd been introduced at the wedding dinner, to everyone there.

How could she forget? Perhaps he'd forgotten also?

Okay, so it was over a year ago, and the day was jam-packed, but how did you forget a man like that?

He was very handsome, and that accent... it was delicious. Like the man himself.

Melanie mentally slapped herself. What on earth was wrong with her?

It was dog-tiredness – it had to be. Philippe was a colleague, and she'd do well to remember that. Besides, she'd been cured of men. Jefferson had seen to that.

She closed her eyes and was soon asleep.

Chapter Three

Melanie stretched herself awake.

She'd had the best sleep she'd had for ages. Not having to endure the horrible stress of day-long abuse had already made a difference.

She knew her bank job had taken its toll but hadn't realized how much until now. She'd been walking around zombie-like before, tossing and turning every night worrying about the abuse she'd cop the next day at work.

Friday and Saturday nights were the only time she slept well, knowing she didn't have to work the next day.

She slid around and sat at the side of the bed, stretched again, then headed for the shower. She couldn't wait to get to work again - a thought she hadn't had for some time.

She arrived half an hour early, putting her bag in her locker. She looped the lanyard around her neck and headed to the break room where she sat down, preparing herself for the day ahead.

"Good morning, Melanie." Philippe leaned in and placed a coffee on the table in front of her and sitting opposite. "I saw you arrive," he said to her wordless query.

"If you have some time today, can you let me know? We have a wedding booked, and we need to coordinate on it."

"Oh?"

"No one told you." It was a statement, not a question. "You will be managing all major events as part of your position. Is that a problem?"

"No, not at all. Cassie did mention events, but not weddings specifically. Let me check my schedule for today and I'll get back to you. Avoiding meal-times of course."

"Thank you, I appreciate that," he said. "Because meal-times are *chahut* – bedlam." He grinned then quickly left the room.

Mel finished her coffee, then headed to the front desk ready to greet the new guests arriving today.

Cassie had mentioned there were a lot of high-profile guests. Many were drawn by the fact they could say they'd stayed in a genuine nineteenth century inn. She looked around. It certainly had appeal.

She glanced outside to see a shiny black limousine pull up. The valet was there, quick as a flash, helping their newly arrived guests.

As they entered, the valet organized their luggage. Mel took a deep breath. She didn't want to stuff this up.

"Welcome Prince Abdul," she said, doing a little curtsy. "I'm Melanie Chalmers, and I'll be looking after you during your stay."

"Please, stop with the formalities," he said, outstretching his hand. "I am Abdul. You can drop the Prince bit, he said grinning. "It is very nice to meet you, Miss Chalmers."

"Melanie, please."

She led him to the front desk, personally organizing his room keys, and that of his entourage, then walked him to the elevator and escorted him to his room.

The Prince had the Executive Suite, and she ensured everything was as it should be before leaving him. She stopped in the doorway before closing the door.

"Can I send up some refreshments? You've traveled a long way."

He nodded his head. "That would be appreciated. Thank you."

Mel closed the door behind her and leaned against the wall with relief. She had got through it and hadn't stuffed it up.

She grinned. Maybe she would get through an entire week of no stuff-ups.

She made her way to the kitchen. "Do you have anything fit for a Prince?" she asked Philippe.

He stared at her blandly. "Do you mean fit for a King?"

"Actually, it's for Prince Abdul in the Executive Suite. An elaborate morning tea would be lovely."

He grinned. "I know. I was just teasing you."

He rolled a tray toward her and opened a silver cover. "Voila." He clicked his fingers and laughed. "I am well prepared. Let me organize the beverages and we shall depart."

Now it was her turn to stare. "You didn't think we could have a lowly attendant serve the prince, did you?"

His cheeky grin told her he was playing with her. "Sierra and I always did this together. So now it's you and me."

They made their way up to the Executive Suite, where Mel knocked lightly on the door. "It's Melanie Chalmers," she said gently.

He opened the door wide to allow the room service tray entrance. "Ah, Chef Philippe. So nice to see you again."

Mel let out the breath she didn't realize she'd been holding.

"Tell me," he asked. "Did Sierra have her baby yet?"

They spent the next few minutes chatting about Cody, then left Prince Abdul in peace with his refreshments.

Another hurdle over and done with. Mel hoped she got through with flying colors.

* * *

They sat side by side in Philippe's office, which was conveniently off the kitchen. "The wedding is this weekend."

Melanie swallowed. She had less than a week to organize a wedding?

Philippe gently touched her arm. "It is no problem," he said in that enticing accent she'd come to love. "We've known about it for some

28

months. Today, you and I, we are confirming the details. Because you are new, I wanted to go over everything with you.”

She nodded hoping he knew what he was doing, because right now, she had no idea.

“The wedding reception will be held in the reception hall, which is where all such events are held.” He rifled through a bundle of papers and pulled out two pages which he placed on the table. “This is the menu we’re using, already approved by the bride and groom.”

Mel studied the menu. It was top notch.

“You need to meet with the happy couple in the next day or two and confirm all the details.”

She glanced around the tiny office. Her glance fell on a photograph of a woman with a baby. She wondered who they were. He didn’t wear a wedding band. *His sister perhaps?*

Her handed her another sheet of paper. “This is a tentative staff roster for the day – you’ll need to go over it and confirm with the staff rostered they are still available.”

Mel worried her bottom lip. Could she really pull this off?

Philippe gazed into her eyes. “You can do this, I *promesse* – promise.” His hand gently touched her shoulder, and he stood, effectively ending their meeting. "Let me know if you need any help. Most of the work is already done, so this one is not so hard. But the next one..." He let his words hang in the air.

"The next one?" Mel's heart thudded. She so couldn't do this.

"Three weeks later. Last weekend in May." His expression dared her to fold. "We shall start work on that one as soon as we have this one organized."

He packed up the rest of the papers and attached them to his clipboard, placing it on the wall. "We have a retirement party in between, but it is nothing." He waved his hands about. "Very easy to organize. You'll see."

Would she have taken this job if she knew about the wedding organization? More than likely.

"It will get easier," he said. "When you've done a few, it will be second nature."

"Done a few?" *What had she let herself in for?*

"We have at least two weddings every month." Philippe said it as though it was no big deal. "It's usually a package deal – the wedding reception and the Bridal Suite. There are usually also room bookings from some of the guests."

"Oh."

"It's generally very, shall we say…*busy* on those days?" His eyes sparkled and he threw back his head in laughter, then just as quickly pulled himself up. "I apologize, Madame," he said jovially. "It really is not funny. But you will get used to it."

"Now, I must go. It starts to get busy again with afternoon tea." He turned toward the kitchen, then stopped. "Shall we meet again this afternoon?" he tossed back over his shoulder.

"This afternoon?"

"For our private rendezvous? Like yesterday?"

She smiled. She couldn't help herself. She patted her belly. "I don't know if my figure will thank you, but yes, that would be lovely, thank you."

"Then I shall see you same time, same place." His grin lit up his face. "Once you have the menu confirmed, let me know so I can order the supplies."

Mel gathered up all the papers relevant to the wedding and went to her own office. Like any new job, it was hard at the beginning, she knew that. Once she got used to it all, it would become second nature.

As she walked away, Mel wondered about her relationship with Philippe. They hadn't known each other long, but it was a comfortable rapport. Very friendly.

Perhaps too friendly?

She'd started off this way with Jefferson. He'd worked at the bank too. She saw no problem with them being friends, *just friends*, but he'd seen it as much more than that.

She didn't.

She flopped down into the chair and rifled through her desk, forcing her mind back to the job at hand.

There had to be a booking diary somewhere, surely?

It seemed to appear out of nowhere, and she opened it tentatively, worried about what she would find there.

She quickly turned to today's date, then flicked over to Saturday's wedding and beyond. Her eyes scanned the dates. Five more weddings were booked over the next few months. She didn't dare look any further.

Blood coursed through her veins and pounded through her head. She needed to get on top of this. Weddings would be a huge boon to the inn, so she had to get it right. She owed it to Brax and Sierra.

As she was about to close the diary, she noticed a piece of paper hiding at the front of the book. She slowly opened it and read it, then smiled.

That was just like Sierra.

In Sierra's own handwriting were instructions on how she organized past weddings, where to find additional information, and which staff were usually available on those days.

She put the note aside and searched the drawers. If there was one note, would there be more?

She sat back in relief when she found a whole notebook full of helpful instructions. Mel wondered why Sierra hadn't mentioned them, but her mind was probably focused on her beautiful baby boy.

Tackling one thing at a time, she read through the instructions, making her own notes as she did so.

Mel put her hands to her chest. Thank goodness Sierra had the forethought to leave this information for her.

The phone rang. "Melanie Chalmers. How may I help you?"

She listened carefully. "Of course Prince, er Abdul. I'll be right up." She replaced the receiver and headed up to help her guest.

Chapter Four

M el stood at the entrance to the inn, feeling a little more weary than she'd hoped. Or perhaps it was anxiety?

Today was the wedding day. Her first.

Philippe stood by her side, which was reassuring.

She had personally checked the Bridal Suite and had sprinkled pale pink rose petals over the bed. After the reception, she would ensure a bottle of champagne and box of chocolates were delivered to the suite.

Sierra's voice echoed in her head – *it's the little things*.

A white limousine pulled up and the valet quickly attended to the bride and groom who had not long left the church after the ceremony.

"Congratulations," she told them enthusiastically, handing the bride a single pink rose. "I am Melanie Chalmers, Guest Services Manager. The Bridal Suite is ready, and I will personally escort you to your room. Your luggage will be delivered to your room shortly."

Philippe stepped forward. "I am Chef Philippe and have prepared your bridal reception. Please speak to Melanie or myself if you have any concerns."

He reached over and took the bride's hand and kissed it gently.

He certainly knew how to win hearts.

"Now I must return to the kitchen." He bowed slightly and began to leave but turned around at the last minute. "I shall send up some refreshments shortly. On the house of course - our wedding gift to you both."

The bride beamed. Little did she know it was included in every bridal package.

True to her promise, Mel escorted the happy couple to their room. It was stunning. She'd been there before when she sprinkled the petals, but now stood at the door and looked around in awe.

It was such a romantic room, and she could only imagine being a new bride and coming here. It would be magical.

This suite was huge compared to the regular rooms. It had silk sheets and pillowcases, as well as a silk-covered duvet. All in white.

The matching curtains were only for show as there were blinds to block out the light, but the curtains gave uniformity to the room.

The large built-in robe was perfect, and allowed their luggage to be out of sight, as was the white sofa that sat in the adjoining lounge room.

The nineteenth century canopy as a finishing touch put a very romantic spin on it all. The thought went through Mel's head as she closed the door behind her guests.

Sierra had certainly thought of everything.

As she stepped out of the elevator, Philippe greeted her.

"One hour until the guests begin to arrive," he said. "Shall we do a last-minute check to ensure everything is running to plan?"

"I'm sure it will be," she said sweetly, then headed to the reception hall with Philippe by her side.

As she predicted, everything was as it should be. Perfection.

They wandered around the room, inspecting each table, one by one.

In the center of each table was a replica of an old-fashioned lantern with a candle instead of a wick. Each one sat on a rustic piece of wood and was surrounded by a selection of flowers, including pale pink roses, forget-me-nots, and a selection of small white flowers and a touch of green foliage.

"It looks so lovely," she said quietly, feeling a little nostalgic.

She strolled over to the Bridal Table. It was the same, only more so. She wondered how many more times she'd stand here like this. Next time she would have more input and would feel more connected.

"It is a work of beauty, no?"

She startled and looked across at him. "Yes, it is. Thanks to you and the wonderful staff who have more than an inkling of what they're doing than I do."

Did he understand how truly grateful she felt? Or how inadequate?

He stared at her as though he could read her thoughts. "Back to the kitchen then." He bowed slightly and turned to leave.

"Philippe," she called after him.

He spun around. "Yes, Madame?"

"Thank you. I couldn't have pulled this off without you."

His faced softened, and his lips lifted into a smile. "You are very welcome." He reached for her hand and kissed it gently. Electricity shot up her arm.

"Now I must away! The sous-chef, he is very good, but he is not Philippe!" He grinned before he disappeared out of sight.

It was nearly time for the other guests to arrive, and Mel decided to have a quick break now or she may not get one. The inn would soon be full of wedding guests for the weekend – it was certainly going to test her abilities.

She flopped down into her office chair and forced herself to relax. In less than half an hour she would be bombarded with guests. Many of whom may need her assistance.

Her phone rang.

"The first guests have arrived," the receptionist told her. Melanie sighed and put on her best smile, ready to greet her latest guests.

* * *

T he reception went well. Melanie spent the

entire time supervising to ensure everything ran smoothly.

Not that she really needed to – her staff were well trained and undeniably knew what they were doing.

The bride looked incredible in her elegant dress, and Melanie watched as the newly weds swayed together on the beautifully restored dance floor.

One day that might be her…

She chased the thought away. She was a confirmed spinster, and besides, she didn't have a boyfriend. Not that she wanted one, either. Jefferson had seen to that.

She shook the thoughts away. She was happily single, and intended to stay that way.

The music stopped and everyone clapped. The couple returned to the Bridal Table, and more speeches began as dessert was served.

"My brother chose well," the Best Man began. "I'm not so sure about his bride!"

The room erupted in laughter.

"Enjoying yourself?" Philippe spoke quietly, so only she could hear.

She turned toward him. "Yes, but I'm exhausted."

"It will be over soon, then you can rest." He lifted her hand and patted it. "The first is always the hardest."

A zing shot through her at his touch, and she quickly pulled her hand back. "I thought you'd be busy in the kitchen," she said. It wasn't an accusation, but a statement.

"The sous-chef and kitchen hands, I train them well," he said with a grin.

"But they are not Philippe!" she said mockingly, repeating his earlier retort.

He chuckled. "They are not. But they are learning." He winked at her and moved away, shadowing some of the wait staff, ensuring everything was to his high standard.

Melanie watched as he stalked the room, chatting to some of the guests, and bowing to them. No doubt soaking up all the compliments on *his* meals. The ones he most likely didn't cook.

Huh!

He certainly did have an ego. With time, she'd probably get used to it. But right now, it grated on her a little.

As soon as all the desserts were served, the wait staff began to serve platters of cheese, crackers, and fruit, then offered tea and coffee to each guest.

What Melanie would do for a coffee right now. Instead she headed for the kitchen to see what she could do to help.

"It is all under control, Madame," Philippe told her with an exaggerated bow. "See these people," he indicated with his hands. "They are all experienced with the weddings. No, you rest, and let them do the work."

He pulled her aside. "That's what we pay them for, Melanie," he said quietly, winking as he did.

Her name rolled off his tongue so beautifully and she wished he used it more. His French accent made it sound so special. Not like an ordinary Melanie, but a Melanie who was to be treasured.

She felt the heat creep up her face.

"What are you thinking," he said laughing. "You are blushing."

"Nothing," she said. "Nothing at all." She began to rush from the room.

How embarrassing. She wasn't sure she would be able to face him again after that little episode. At least he had no idea what made her blush.

"Melanie," he called after her. "Wait up," he said softly. "You were thinking about me, weren't you?" He had a cocky grin on his face.

The nerve of the man.

He had her cornered near the exit to the reception hall, but she didn't feel any fear. She knew Philippe had no bad intentions toward her.

"Okay, you got me. But it's not what you think," she said. She licked her lipstick covered lips and he stared down at them. "I liked the way my name sounds with your accent," she said nervously.

He smirked but said nothing.

"Happy now?" she said, then began to walk away.

"It is kind of sexy, my accent, no?" He continued to smirk, and she felt like slapping him.

"I have to go," she said, beginning to move away.

"Mel-an-ie," he said slowly. "Yes, I like how it sounds."

Her heart pounded in her chest – from her annoyance of course. There was no other reason.

She stared into his brown puppy eyes and couldn't pull her glance away. She licked her lips again. "I, I have to go," she said urgently. And she truly did. Had to get away before she did something she might regret.

Philippe had a pull on her that no one else ever had.

Chapter Five

It had been a long day.

A very long day. And now she was ready to go home.

She stood in the locker-room and snatched up her bag, then flaked against the wall, closing her eyes as she did so.

"Melanie, you are still here."

She'd know that voice anywhere.

"Philippe," she said flatly. She just wanted to go home and collapse into bed.

"You look exhausted, my friend."

She opened her eyes and looked sideways at him. *Well duh!* She'd been here since early this morning, and now it was dark outside. *Of course she was exhausted!*

"I look exhausted, because I am exhausted," she said softly. "I just want to get out of here."

"Melanie," he said, playing on the fact she liked how he said her name. "I have a surprise for you."

He hooked his arm through hers and warmth spread through her body. "Where are we going?"

Despite her reluctance, she let him lead her.

They walked through the reception room where the function had been in full swing just a short time ago. The staff had almost finished cleaning it up, and it looked like a totally different place now.

"Nuh, uh. It won't be a surprise if I tell you." That cocky grin reared its head once more. But she couldn't say it upset her. In fact, she kinda liked it.

It was cute.

She mentally slapped herself. What on earth was she thinking? It just proved how tired she really was.

Philippe led her into the restaurant which was empty of guests at this time of the night.

In the middle of the room was a small table.

The center of the table had a candle burning, and the lights were down low. A bottle of champagne was sitting on ice.

He pulled out the chair and helped her into it, then uncorked the champagne.

Handing her a glass, his eyes never left hers. "Tonight we celebrate," he said. "Just the two of us."

He then poured himself a glass. "To the two of us – we make a great team." He clinked his glass to hers and began to drink.

"Thanks," she said quietly. Champagne was nice, but a sleep would be even nicer.

Philippe pouted. "You are not happy, my Melanie."

"I'm tired. Really, really tired."

He frowned. "I thought to make you a bite to eat."

She shook her head. She really just wanted to go to bed.

"Ah, but you must eat. You are too skinny already – I mean to fatten you up." He winked at her and grinned.

That lopsided grin of his got her every time.

She sighed. "Okay, you win."

"*Bien*. Good. Wait here." He headed toward the kitchen, and Melanie's curiosity was peaked.

He returned a short time later with a plate of entrées. They looked appetizing. "Excess from the wedding. But perfectly good," he said. "We always make extra, just in case of the accidents."

She loved his accent. Melanie didn't care what he said, his words practically sang in her mind.

He pushed the plate toward her. "Go on, take some. But beware, some are hot." He handed her a napkin and passed over a small plate as well.

He pointed to each item. "Cheese and bacon stuffed mushrooms, scallops wrapped in bacon, smoked salmon with feta and pine nuts, and roasted red capsicum bruschetta."

She reached for a stuffed mushroom and took a bite. "Mmmm, heaven."

Philippe lifted a napkin and touched it her mouth. The buzz she felt left her reeling.

He stared into her eyes. "You had a little cheese..." He pointed to the corner of her mouth.

She didn't want to acknowledge what had just happened but felt she should. "Thank you. The food is amazing, but I must go."

He leaned back in his seat, disappointment evident in his expression. "I am sorry, Melanie,' he said. "I overstepped the mark. Don't go – you are hungry, and I have delicious food here for you."

She glanced at him and then at the food. He was right, she needed to eat, and this wonderful food would end up in the rubbish if they didn't eat it. "Okay. Okay, I'll stay, but perhaps we need to set some rules?"

He rubbed his hand across the dark stubble that was now showing on his chin. "I like you Melanie,"

She interrupted. "I like you too, but…"

"But we work together. I understand." He pushed his fingers through his wavy black hair. "More is the pity. We are good together."

"We are," she said quietly, then picked up a piece of the bruschetta. This food was to die for. "It's not you," she said softly, avoiding his eyes at all cost. She closed her eyes, trying to push the bad memories to the back of her mind, but it only made them worse.

She opened them suddenly, panic beginning to rise. She startled when Philippe gently touched her hand.

"Are you alright my friend?" Concern was written all over his face.

She straightened her back and brushed his words away. "I'm fine," she said. "Don't mind me." She picked up a scallop and popped it in her mouth. "Mmmm, amazing. Do we get to do this after every wedding?"

He laughed and pushed the plate further toward her. "If that's what you want, we most definitely will."

* * *

When they'd had their fill of wedding cuisine, including a selection of cold desserts, Philippe had walked Melanie to her car.

It was dark, and despite her protests, there was no way he'd allow her to go out alone. The tiny outback town of Oakdale was usually safe, but you just never knew. He wasn't going to risk her safety.

She'd offered to help him clean up, but he'd refused the offer. That's what dishwashers are for, he'd told her jokingly.

It made her laugh, which made him happy. He'd been very concerned earlier when she'd had a panic attack; it seems to come out of nowhere. One minute she'd closed her eyes, only momentarily, and suddenly she was in panic mode.

He frowned. What had done that to his Melanie?

He gasped. She wasn't *his Melanie*, and he had to cleanse himself of those thoughts.

What would Amelie say? He shook himself.

He muddled about in the kitchen for a while, doing a lot of nothing, and decided it was time to go home. He'd be back at work before he knew it, and he wanted to spend as much time with Amelie as he could. Their time together was precious.

He removed his chef's jacket, then turned off the lights to the kitchen and restaurant and headed for the main entrance.

"Goodnight, Faith," he muttered to the receptionist as he left. "Enjoy your evening." He gave her a brief wave and headed for his own car.

When he arrived home, he entered quietly, and headed straight to check on Amelie. He watched her sleeping and wondered what he'd done to deserve this beautiful creature. He leaned in and gently kissed her forehead.

"Goodnight, *mon amour*," he said in a whisper, ensuring not to wake her. Tomorrow

was his day off, and he would relish every second
of their time together.

Chapter Six

Melanie awoke with a start.

She glanced over at the bedside clock and gasped.

10am.

She flew out of bed, headed for the bathroom and reached for the shower taps. Then remembered it was her day off. She turned herself around and climbed back into bed, pulling the still-warm covers around her.

She'd had the best sleep last night. Better than she'd had for months, and she put it down to her change of job.

No more worrying about abuse. No more nasty customers.

She sighed contentedly.

Sure, she'd had a busy week, and she'd been on the go the whole time. Her brain was in overload from everything she'd had to learn, but she was still under less stress than she had been at the bank.

She closed her eyes and tried to go back to sleep but sleep totally alluded her now.

She finally dragged herself out of bed and wrapped her robe around herself, rubbing the sleep out of her eyes. She filled the kettle with water, then flopped down at the table.

Coffee finally in her hands, she stared out the kitchen window. She loved her little unit, even if it was in town. Braxton had tried to cajole her into moving out of town and closer to him.

But she liked living where she did. It was close to everything – she could walk to work, and did so most days, but not when she had to come home in the dark.

Thinking about work led to thinking about Philippe, which was not what she wanted.

She told herself Jefferson was the reason she refused to get close to Philippe, or any man for that matter, and in some ways that was true.

If she stopped lying to herself, the real truth was she was scared. Too afraid to give her heart to someone else. Someone who might turn out to be the opposite to what he initially seemed.

Was Philippe that man? She didn't think so, but she didn't really know him. After all, she'd only known him for a week.

It was obvious the two of them hit it off. And she reacted every time he touched her. Did he feel it too? If he did, she wasn't aware of it.

Besides, they worked together. What happened if they began a relationship then broke it off?

She sipped her coffee trying to push her thoughts aside. They were way out of control.

A relationship with Philippe would be ludicrous. Apart from the obvious, she didn't even know the man. Was he married, was he single, was he even a nice person?

He seemed nice enough – at work – but it was easy to hide your true personality. Jefferson was proof of that.

Thank goodness for Braxton…

She shook herself. This was not a conversation she wanted to have with herself. Melanie lifted the mug to her lips and took a huge mouthful, then continued to stare out the window.

Life as a single woman suited her perfectly, and that's exactly how she intended to remain.

* * *

Melanie sat at her desk feeling totally stress-free after two days off. Two days of relaxation. She couldn't ask for anything more.

Her phone began to trill, but it no longer bothered her like it had at the bank.

"Melanie Chalmers." She wrote notes as she listened carefully. "This Saturday?" She drew in a breath. "I will have to confer with our head chef before I can commit to that and will get back to you shortly."

And so it begins again. But this time the organization was solely on her. She knew it would happen but had no idea it would be so soon.

She picked up the phone to call the kitchen. They wouldn't have face-to-face contact if she could help it.

It rang several times before he picked up. "This is Philippe." His strong accent sent a delicious shiver through her.

"Good morning," she said. "It's Melanie."

He chuckled down the line. "I know, it came up on the screen. Good morning to you too. What can I do for you, Melanie?" He emphasized her name, drawing it out. Solely for her benefit she was certain.

Was he doing it on purpose just to annoy her?

"I have a last-minute request for a function on Saturday. Can we accommodate?"

"Provided there is no other booking, we will always accommodate function requests," he told her. "You are new," he said. "But for future reference, we never turn function bookings away."

She felt her face go red and was glad they weren't in the same room. She'd messed up royally.

"Do not berate yourself, Melanie," he said, as though he could read her mind. "Call them back and organise a time this afternoon or in the morning. We'll be on our toes, but we can manage."

"Thank Philippe."

They said their goodbyes, and she disconnected the call, then called back the potential client. They'd never used the inn before, so this could be good for future business too.

After she'd made all the arrangements, she pulled out the notebook Sierra had left for her and began to read over them.

She could do this. Sierra had confidence in her, and so did Philippe.

She slunk down in her office chair. They had far more confidence in her abilities than she did.

"Ah, Melanie," Philippe said, tucking his head around her office door. "Coffee for you – I'm sure you can use it. How did you go with the client?"

She straightened up in her seat. "Thanks for the coffee." She really needed it but didn't need the zing she got when their hands brushed. "They'll be here at 2.30 – I hope that is okay for you."

"*Oui*. Yes, it is fine." He handed her a clipboard. "Some food suggestions. We'll go over this with the client this afternoon, but this is...." He waved his hands in the air. "a start. We go from there. My staff, they are organised. Tentatively. Yours?"

"Oh." She hadn't given that a thought, but she should have. It was only five days away.

She pulled some previous rosters out of the drawer and went over them. "I'll get on it right away." She'd already begun contacting staff before Philippe had left the room. It wasn't a lot of notice, but they had to be sure to cover the event.

She finally got off the phone an hour later and printed off the staff roster. It was a lot of work, especially being her first time doing this from scratch, but it would be worth it.

Melanie leaned back in her chair and relaxed.

"Melanie," It was Cassie, the inn manager this time. "We've just got word we'll have a movie celebrity and his entourage joining us tomorrow. Here are all the details." She handed Melanie a list, then left.

This job sure kept her busy, but she wouldn't have it any other way.

* * *

"There are two ways we can do this," Melanie explained. "Either way we'll have everyone seated at the tables. We can provide set meal, or a buffet. It depends on your requirements." She handed Peter Janson a clipboard.

"We have made up two suggested menus, one for each type. If you have any specific requirements, we can of course, include those."

Janson scrutinized the menu and frowned.

Melanie and Philippe glanced at each other. Was he going to back out now?

He looked up, still frowning. "Now I don't know which way to go," he said. "I hadn't thought about a buffet at all."

She felt herself relax. "It really depends on whether you want people wandering around while the proceedings continue," she said.

He shook his head. "No. No, I really don't. We'll have high profile guest speakers, and I don't want them distracted." He studied the menus again and spoke directly to Philippe. "You'll be able to cater for dietary and religious requirements?"

"Definitely," Philippe said. "Get a list to me by Friday and we can comply."

"Good." Peter Janson stood. "I'll see you Saturday then." He reached over and shook Philippe's hand, then turned to Melanie.

"I'm sorry to have to ask Mr Janson,"

"Peter, please."

"Peter it is. Because it is such short notice, and we'll have to get in all the supplies almost immediately, we'll need full payment up front.'

"Oh, of course you do. I do apologise." He reached into his wallet and pulled out a credit card, handing it to Melanie.

"If you'll follow me to the main office and we'll get this processed."

"I'll leave you to it," Philippe said. "I look forward to doing more business with you in the future, Peter."

The men shook hands, and they all turned to leave the conference room. Philippe put his hand to her back, and a thrill went down her spine. Until then, she'd been able to keep it all business. If she wasn't careful, she might start having feelings for this man with his sexy French accent.

All Melanie wanted to do right now was get far away from him. Her heart was being sorely tested, and she wanted it to stop.

Chapter Seven

Another busy day.

Melanie had come to realize that's how this job was always going to be.

She wasn't complaining.

She said a silent prayer of thanks to Sierra and Braxton for offering her this unique opportunity.

"Good morning, Melanie." She looked up to see Philippe with his lopsided smile standing over her. As always, he held out a coffee to her.

"You spoil me, Philippe." She reached out to take the offered beverage. "Oh, there's a little cookie too. Thank you," she said grinning. "What a pleasant surprise."

He shrugged. "I got bored in the kitchen and started playing. I thought *why not?*"

There was that lopsided grin again – it got her every time.

"Our guests," he said, "will get a pleasant surprise today. Between we two, I made these especially for you."

Her breath caught in her throat. "For me?" she squeaked, then cleared her throat. What had he been thinking?

As though he could read her thoughts he frowned. "I don't think you understand how special you are, Melanie." His hands flourished across in front of him, the he leaned down and whispered in her ear. "You are *extraordinaire*."

Her jaw dropped, but he was gone before she could respond. Quiet as a panther stalking its prey, and twice as dangerous.

She took a sip of the perfect cappuccino that had been delivered by the inn's head chef. And a thought popped into her head. *Why didn't he send one of the kitchen hands if all he wanted was to give her coffee?*

But she already knew the answer. They had a connection and he had to see her. She understood because as much as she fought it, she felt exactly the same way about him.

It was like an itch that needed to be scratched – it was hell and heaven all at the same time.

She shut her eyes and squeezed them tight, rolling her shoulders. She was a problem solver from way back, but she couldn't see a solution to this one.

She opened her eyes and stared down into her coffee, breathing in the aroma, then took another sip. She eyed the tiny cookie sitting on the side of the small plate – she'd resisted for too long.

Popping it in her mouth, Melanie relished the exquisite taste of it. She wondered if Philippe had been toying with her when he said he'd made them just for her.

She shook her head. Surely he hadn't done that.

But she wanted to know.

Reaching for the phone to find out, she shook her head again and dropped the receiver. She wouldn't embarrass herself by asking.

She looked up when she heard a quiet knock on her open door.

Melanie gazed at the man. She'd seen him before but didn't really know him. He was in a kitchen uniform, so he obviously worked for Philippe.

"Good morning, Ma'am," he said, his arms outstretched. "This is a gift from Chef."

She looked at his name badge. Adam. "Thank you, Adam." Checking over the gift, she discovered a small plate of tiny cookies, just like the one Philippe had given her. She smiled.

He turned to leave.

"Please thank Philippe for me," she said to his retreating back.

He turned back to her and nodded, a huge grin on his face. *Did he know something she didn't?* She shrugged it off, not wanting to go there.

Once Adam was out of sight, Melanie checked her watch. Another half hour and their movie celebrity and his entourage would be arriving. A call to housekeeping ensured their rooms were ready.

Philippe would be on the ball and would have their welcome trolley ready, apart from the beverages. The inn ran like a well-oiled piece of machinery, and it made her smile.

Unlike the bank where nothing could be predicted or expected. Some days it was utter chaos.

She drank down the last of her coffee and finalized the rosters for the event on Saturday. She then emailed a copy to each relevant staff member.

She ticked rosters off her long list of things to do before Saturday.

Her phone rang again. After announcing herself she listened carefully. "I'll just check the diary for you." She flicked the pages and found the appropriate date. "That date *is* available," she said, picking up her pencil.

She heard the bride-to-be squeal and smiled.

"I'm afraid we don't have a garden where you can be married." She heard the disappointment on the other end. "Your wedding is not for some months. Let me make some enquiries and I'll get back to you. No promises." Another squeal.

She hoped she wasn't going to disappoint the excited bride-to-be. "It might take a week or two." She listened careful. "Yes, I have you penciled in, and no, no one else will get your date once your deposit is paid."

She picked up the phone and called Cassie, the inn manager. She explained the dilemma, and Cassie told her she was welcome to explore the possibility. Since she was Guest Services Manager, the task fell to her.

Cassie also suggested she discuss it with Philippe since it would also affect him, especially if he was expected to serve hors d'oeuvres in the garden.

Melanie stiffened her shoulders at this news, but at the same time a thrill went through her.

"Shall we meet for lunch and discuss it?" he asked after they'd welcomed their celebrity guest. "I shall supply the food."

After the lunch rush, Philippe collected her from her office, then led her through the front entrance.

"It's a beautiful day," he said, answering her unspoken question. "I thought we'd walk to the park and eat there. I've made some sandwiches, petit quiches, and also have *un sachet de petits cadeaux.*"

She stared at him.

"Apologies, Madame. A little bag of goodies. Sweet goodies."

Melanie wished she could remember some of the French language she'd learned at school. At the time she thought it would be totally useless in the real world. Little did she know.

The Oakdale Public Park wasn't far. It was a pleasant ten-minute walk, and they began chatting about Melanie's idea.

Philippe put a hand to his chin, which he often did when he was contemplating something. He nodded his head tentatively. "Perhaps," he said. "It might be *possible.*"

She adored when he dropped in a French word. Especially when she understood it. And possible was the same in both languages, just with a different accent. She almost laughed out loud. She could be ridiculous sometimes.

"Ah, we are here." He put his hand to her back and led her to a park bench. A thrill went down her spine. She mentally slapped herself. Hadn't she decided to make herself immune from the sexy French chef?

She glanced around the park she never really looked at. It had been years since Melanie had been here. She'd cut through it when she was running late, but hadn't really seen it. She'd always been in too much of a rush.

There was a small pond with a fence around it. The large children's playground beyond it explained the necessity for the fence. Beyond that was a garden. It was far from botanical gardens, but even from this distance she could see how pretty and appealing it would be to walk through on a sunny day.

She'd have to make the time to come here again soon.

As they snacked on their casual lunch, they talked about the wedding garden possibility. Philippe nodded when appropriate and gave his opinion on whether or not various elements would be feasible.

"I really like your idea, Melanie," he said, rolling her name off his tongue in that magical way only Philippe could do. "I also think it could be very profitable for the inn."

He took a deep breath. "But…"

"Papa!!"

A little voice squealed from the children's playground. When she glanced up, a child of around four was running toward them.

Melanie couldn't see anyone else this child would be running toward.

Philippe was beaming. "Amelie! What a wonderful surprise." He embraced the little girl, pulling her up into his lap. He looked across the park and waved to a woman who was walking toward them.

"Melanie," he said, looking a little sheepish. "This is my daughter, Amelie."

Philippe had a daughter? Did that mean he was married? All kinds of thoughts were running through her mind, not all of them nice.

But that wasn't the child's fault.

"Hello, Amelie," she said sweetly. "How old are you? I'll bet you're two," she said teasingly.

Amelie laughed. "No silly, I'm four. I'm a *big* girl!" She pointed at her chest as she emphasized the word big.

Melanie laughed at the child's antics. Amelie reached up and put her arms around Philippe's neck. Her father's neck.

"I missed you, Papa," she said with a French accent.

He squeezed his eyes closed as he hugged his daughter tight. "I missed you too, *mon amour*," he whispered.

Melanie studied his face; his pain was apparent. If he had the choice, she knew he'd choose to spend his time with this sweet little girl.

Amelie pulled back and stared into his face, her little hands holding each of his cheeks. "Papa," she said excitedly. "Papa..." She was so animated, and Melanie couldn't understand a word she said. It was quite bewildering.

"Amelie," he said gently. "English please. It is very rude to talk in French when Melanie cannot understand."

She watched with horror as the child's eyes filled with tears. "I'm sorry, Madame," she said, tears streaming down her little face. "I didn't want to be rude."

She tucked her little head on her father's shoulder and sobbed. He patted her back gently. "It is alright. No need for tears."

Melanie was mesmerized by Philippe with a child on his knee. This was a whole knew side to the man she thought she knew. This scenario reinforced her belief you could never truly know a person.

Amelie brushed her tears away with the back of her hand, then turned to her father again, glancing across at Melanie too, not sure who to direct her words at. "We saw ducks," she said, flapping her arms like wings, and wriggling to get down. "They walk like this, Papa!"

She waddled about in front of them, going around and around in circles.

"Are you a duck, Amelie? I wonder if ducks like cookies?" He glanced across to Melanie and winked.

She stopped in her tracks and came running for a cookie. She was such a cutie.

Melanie loved kids, provided they weren't her own and she could hand them back. Like Sierra and Braxton's baby, Cody. She didn't mind babysitting, because at the end of the night, she could walk away, back to her own peaceful unit.

She didn't see herself as a nurturing kind of person. Besides, she was a career woman, and wasn't even slightly interested in having children.

She shivered. She couldn't think of anything worse.

"Duckie wants another cookie, please." Amelie began to quack like a duck until given a cookie. She was way too cute.

"Melanie," Philippe said, as the woman finally reached them. "This is my sister, Danielle. She is Amelie's live-in nanny."

Her eyes opened wide. A live-in nanny? She was more confused than ever.

She watched as Danielle's eyebrows rose, silently questioning her brother.

Melanie tried to ignore the gesture, wondering what it meant, then extended her hand.

"Melanie and I work together," he told his sister blandly, and the women exchanged pleasantries.

Philippe checked his watch.

"I'm sorry little one, but Papa and Melanie have to go back to work."

The little girl pouted, and Melanie was sure those little brown eyes were going to fill with tears again.

"We could walk with you?" Danielle whispered, but little ears heard every word.

Father and daughter both grinned. "Excellent!" Philippe lifted his daughter up onto his shoulders and they headed back to the inn. Melanie had a lot of questions, but now was not the time.

Besides, was it really any of her business? Philippe would have told her if he'd wanted her to know.

When they arrived, he lifted her down again and gave her a huge heartfelt hug. "Don't go, Papa. Please," she pleaded.

But he had to go, and Melanie could see regret written all over his face.

"Papa must go," he told Amelie. "Otherwise lots of people will be hungry."

She nodded her little head, and walked sadly away with her aunt.

When they were alone again, Philippe took her by the shoulders. "I have much to explain," he said in a similar tone he'd used on his daughter – soft and gentle.

"You don't owe me an explanation," she said, shrugging out of his grip and turning toward her office. "It has absolutely nothing to do with me."

She was hurt that he'd kept something so important from her, but at least now she knew they could never be together. He was married with a child.

But still one thing niggled at her – if he was married, why did he have a live-in nanny?

She shook the thought away and vowed to keep Philippe and his amazingly sexy voice to the deep dungeons of her mind.

Later that afternoon Philippe ducked his head around her office door. "I come bearing gifts."

He normally arrived with a huge grin on his face. Not this time.

"Sure," she said coldly. It came out more abruptly than she intended. She was determined to keep her distance from him. They had become too personal; had gotten way too close in the short time they'd known each other.

He carried a tray with two coffees and an assortment of pastries. She cleared a space on her desk for him to set them down. *What was she doing? She should be discouraging him, not making him feel welcome.*

"This is a peace offering," he said, passing one of the coffees to Melanie.

She took a sip. "I love peace offerings," she said. "Especially when they involve chocolate eclairs." She grinned at him, then remembered she was supposed to be distancing herself.

He snatched up a serviette from the tray, then reached out and gently wiped her top lip.

The gesture sent a zap of electricity right through her. He stared into her eyes. She couldn't pull her gaze away.

They sat there like that for what seemed like hours, but in reality was only a matter of seconds. She finally lifted her hand and wiped her fingers across her lip. It still tingled.

Trying to take the focus off the atmosphere between them, Melanie grabbed one of the pastries and took a bite.

It was delicious. Just as she knew Philippe's kiss would be.

Oh. My. Gosh.

Why did he come here? His presence only proved to torment her, and what a blissful torment it was.

"Perfection, no?"

He was so arrogant, so full of himself. But yes, it was perfection.

She nodded. Her mouth was full, and she wanted to savor the moment. Get every second out of this incredible pastry.

The man was an artiste. This wasn't mere cooking, this was artistry at its best.

She swallowed and her tongue ducked out to wipe away any excess.

Philippe's eyes opened wide. They followed her tongue – he was staring...at her mouth.

Melanie quickly grabbed up her coffee, almost spilling it on herself. "I, I...they're amazing, Philippe," she said, stumbling to get the words out.

"Made by my own hands," he said proudly. "The sous-chef, he is good, but..."

Melanie finished for him. "But he is not Philippe."

They both laughed and lightened the mood.

She looked down at the remaining pastries sitting on the plate between them. "Have more," he said. "There are plenty. If we run out, I take some more from the kitchen, no?" He grinned his lopsided grin.

Her heart beat increased and she knew, despite her resolve, she had a real fight on her hands. Philippe was not the demon she was making him out to be. She just had to hear him out and let him explain.

"Melanie," he said quietly. "We need to talk, I have to explain..."

Cassie Somerton ducked her head around the door. "Oh, sorry," she said, handing Melanie a printed sheet. "This week's bookings. I've highlighted the *special interest* bookings."

"Thanks." Melanie stared after Cassie as she walked away.

"Where was I? Oh yes," Philippe said. He reached out and held her hand in his.

The phone began to trill. "Sorry," she said, genuinely meaning it. "This is pretty much my day."

He dropped her hand and indicated for her to take the call. "Melanie Chalmers," she said confidently. "Can you please repeat the date?" She glanced across at Philippe. She listened carefully; his presence was distracting. "Let me just check."

She put the call on hold.

"I'm sorry, Philippe. I have to deal with this call." She was sorry too. Melanie wanted to sort this out as much as Philippe did. But now wasn't the time or the place.

"Of course," he said as he stood. "I will leave these *des pâtisseries*, er, pastries here for you." He winked then left, leaving Melanie to deal with her booking.

She sat for a moment, letting her heart rate get back to normal. Philippe did to her what she vowed no man would ever do again.

Chapter Eight

Dinner. My place, tonight – 6pm?

Philippe hoped the smiley icon at the end of the email would win her over.

He'd just stood when his computer beeped.

Address?

She'd added a heart icon.

That was enough to force his heart to skip a beat.

He fist-pumped the air. "Yes!"

"You okay, Chef?" Adam stood in the doorway to Philippe's office.

He pulled himself together and straightened his chef's jacket. "Of course. Can I help you, Adam?"

"I hope so. I'm having an issue with the choux pastry." His eyes were downcast.

Philippe sighed inwardly, but knew he shouldn't – choux pastry was difficult. "Did you leave the heat on while adding the flour?"

Adam's face drained of all color, and Philippe felt for him.

"Sorry, Chef. I turned off the heat after the butter and water began to simmer."

It was a rookie problem, but Adam was still learning. Despite that, he was proving to be a star when it came to pastries.

"Bin it and start over. Follow the recipe carefully." Philippe touched his apprentice's shoulder. "You are here to learn, and will learn by your mistakes. You will be a master one day if you work hard – you might even be as good as Philippe!" He laughed at his own words.

The look on Adam's face was reward enough for Philippe. What was a bit of food waste compared to the joy he'd just produced? It was nothing.

He turned the apprentice around and sent him back to his work station.

Philippe wandered about, looking over the shoulders of his sous-chef and kitchen hands, nodding his head in appreciation as he went. By the time he arrived at Adam's work station, he was about to add the flour.

"Is this heat low enough, Chef?" he asked.

Philippe was thoughtful. "What do *you* think? You've done this before."

Adam glanced at him, trying to gauge his opinion. "Yes, it's the right temperature." He began to slowly add the flour and beat it into the melted butter and water mixture.

"Perfection," Philippe said, then went back to his office, leaving Adam to finish his task alone.

He sat at his computer and replied to Melanie's question.

Pick you up at your office? We can go via your place if you want to change.

He added a cute little chef icon.

Philippe felt like a teenager pursuing his first crush. He hadn't dated in years, if you could call this a date, and he was scared out of his mind.

There was so much at stake here, not the least Amelie and how this would affect her.

He sat at his desk and worked out his menu for dinner. Nothing too fancy, but not too plain either. If he started at the top of the ladder, there would be nothing more for him to aspire to.

He grimaced. He was thinking like a crazy man.

He grabbed the sheet of paper and screwed it up, then threw it in the recycle container. Slapping his forehead he realized Melanie wouldn't be expecting something akin to what he'd serve at the inn. Would she?

He shook himself. Of course she wouldn't. He could serve up fish with salad and fries and she'd be happy. At least he thought she would.

So why did his brain fail him when he was trying to come up with a meal plan for tonight? It never had before. He prepared meals for hundreds of people at a time, and did it well. Their weddings were proof of that.

But when it came to impressing, Melanie…

Is that was he was doing? Trying to impress Melanie?

Perhaps. But it was giving him brain freeze.

He wandered out into the kitchen. "Listen up, minions," he said. It was a term of endearment with his staff, and they all knew it. Loved it, in fact. "Two-course meal, quick and simple to prepare, but good enough to impress. Go!"

Notepad in hand, he jotted down all the ideas thrown at him. As he began to return to his office, someone called out. "Hot date tonight, Chef?"

He turned back and grinned. "Perhaps," he said mysteriously, and continued on his journey, a grin still on his face.

* * *

Melanie sat at her desk in anticipation, praying her phone wouldn't ring.

She tidied her desk, checked her diary, and closed down her computer. Then she just sat back and tried to relax.

Philippe should be here any minute.

Her phone rang. She grimaced. She did *not* want to pick it up, but felt compelled to. Checking the display screen she saw it was the man in question. "Hi Philippe," she said brightly.

"I apologize," he said. "I shall be there shortly." Then he hung up.

She grabbed her things and waited in the foyer. Philippe arrived soon after she did.

They walked toward the entrance without a word. The moment they were outside, Melanie let out a sigh. She couldn't believe this was actually happening.

"Did you want to go home and get changed," Philippe asked.

"Yes please. I want to get out of this uniform."

He nodded, then led her to his car. They drove the short distance to Melanie's little unit in silence. "Sit down and make yourself comfortable. I won't be long," she told him, then strolled into her bedroom to change, trying to look as casual as possible.

Little did he know how much turmoil she was experiencing.

She flung open the wardrobe. What should she wear? She pulled out six different outfits and threw them on the bed.

She couldn't make up her mind.

Melanie eventually settled on denims with a soft pink shirt. She snatched up a casual jacket in case it got cool later. She let her hair down and brushed it, then quickly freshened her light make-up. Lastly she slipped into some flat shoes.

As she walked back into the loungeroom, she heard Philippe whistle low.

"That work uniform doesn't do you justice," he said quietly.

She felt the heat rise in her cheeks, but said nothing.

"Are you ready," he asked, moving next to her. "I like your home, by the way," he said as an afterthought. "It's very cozy."

"Thanks. I like it."

He put his hand to the small of her back to lead her outside. It did crazy things to her. Things like the zing that was currently spinning its way up and down her spine, the tingle she felt when his arm brushed against hers. Not to mention the warmth that whooshed through her just having him standing near.

How was she going to survive an entire evening with him being so close?

The little voice inside her head told her to stop lying to herself, she was enjoying it. But another much louder voice told her this was too great a risk to take.

What if he turned out to be like Jefferson? She swallowed hard, and losing concentration, almost tripped. Philippe was there to stop her falling.

Would he always be there for her? Or would he turn out to be like Jefferson, and try to get whatever he could from her?

She turned to look at Philippe. This gentle man with his beguiling accent and his soft demeanor was nothing like Jefferson.

He actually liked her. When Braxton had shielded her and shown Jefferson the door, he'd spat out that he'd never liked her anyway. It stung. She was really hurt at his words, but was more embarrassed that she'd let herself be taken in by a snake like that.

Philippe stared into her eyes. "You have beautiful eyes, *mon amour*," he said softly.

"Thanks," she said, and brushed a stray hair back behind her ear. He would never understand what his words meant to her.

He opened her door before going around to the drivers side. She noted the booster seat in the back. She looked forward to seeing Amelie again. The kid was cute. She had brown eyes, just like her papa.

"We live about fifteen minutes drive out of town," he said. "Not too far. I have to call into the supermarket on our way, if you don't mind."

She nodded.

He laughed. "If you do, you'll starve tonight – I have to pick up some supplies."

Her heart skipped a beat. She loved his funny little ways. The small things he said and did that made her laugh. Made her heart soar.

After parking in a nearby space, they went into the supermarket together. Philippe was particular about his purchases, checking everything carefully.

Melanie stood silently alongside him, taking in everything he did. For a moment she wondered if he was so precise about the inn's supplies, but instinctively knew he would be. The man was a perfectionist.

"I am done," he announced, then headed toward the register. Melanie glanced in the shopping basket, but couldn't work out what he was preparing to cook.

"No peeking," he said jokingly. "It is to be *une surprise.*"

She felt her resistance melt every time he dropped a French word or two. He was everything she'd ever wanted in a man – he was charming, caring, and a real gentleman. And that didn't take into account he was handsome. So very handsome.

As he paid for his purchases, she looked him up and down. From his shoes right up to his curly black hair.

He glanced sideways at her and caught her watching. She felt the heat in her face and was sure she would be as red as a beetroot! *How embarrassing.*

He reached out and put an arm around her shoulders. "Do you like what you see?" he whispered in her ear.

Melanie wanted to run far away and hide. But then she realized he'd done the same thing to her in her unit.

"Just reciprocating," she said boldly.

"Touché." He chuckled as they walked back to the car. He filled the trunk with the supplies, then they were on their way.

"What are you making?" she asked cheekily, knowing he wouldn't tell her.

"No, no, no," he said playfully. "You have to wait and see."

Melanie admired the scenery as they drove toward his property. "Do you like it out here?" she asked. "I know you haven't been here long – only since the inn opened."

"It is wonderful. For Amelie it is an amazing place to grow up. The city? It is not good for children. Here she can run around and play."

"But do *you* like it," she asked again.

"*Oui.* I adore it. Especially the past few weeks." He briefly turned and winked at her as he continued to drive.

She knew exactly what he meant. That's how long they'd known each other.

"My little Amelie, she waits at the gate with aunty Danielle."

Melanie looked up to see child and aunt at the gate. How sweet. Right then she felt a pang to have someone anticipating her arrival home. How great would that be?

Stop it! She wasn't interested in getting married or having children – it was all about her career.

Philippe parked his car, then almost ran to his sweet child. She wondered what it would be like to be so loved by another person.

"Say hello to Melanie." He swept his hand toward her.

"*Bonjour*, Melanie," she said in her little voice, then slapped her hands to her mouth. "I mean, hello."

She wrapped her arms around her father's legs. "It is alright, little one. I'm sure Melanie understands *bonjour*."

She laughed. "High school French. I understand a few words. Can't remember most of it though." She smiled at Amelie, who brightened at the knowledge she wasn't in trouble.

Philippe unpacked the groceries and headed inside. "Come, Melanie," he instructed as she stood at the gate. "Make yourself at home."

Melanie followed him into the spacious kitchen. She'd expected it to be a reasonable size, but not like this.

"I adore your kitchen," she said, looking about.

"*Oui*, I had it custom made before we moved in." He indicated the large windows that took up the width of the kitchen. "These windows too. The view is too beautiful to cover up, no?"

"Yes. Yes it is." She looked out across the valley toward the mountains. No doubt snow covered the peaks in the winter months. "The view is stunning."

He unpacked his groceries and lined them up on the counter. As Melanie watched, she noticed how meticulous he was about where each item was placed.

His lips curled as he noticed her staring. "They are in the order I need them," he said. "We do the same at the inn. It is more...time economical that way."

Ah! That made sense. Perhaps it was something she should think about doing. Melanie's cooking efforts were always so haphazard. When she bothered to cook that was. Frozen dinners and cheese toasties were much more convenient.

"First we sit and spend some time together. Amelie will go to bed soon."

Melanie was surprised. "She's not eating with us?"

The lopsided grin came into play. "We will eat grown up food. Amelie has eaten age-appropriate food earlier. This time of night is too late for such a small child to eat." He raised his eyebrows asking her an unspoken question.

"I have no idea," Melanie said. "I've had little to do with children."

"So it seems." He reached over and patted her hand. "Do not worry. It is of no consequence."

The moment his skin touched hers, a zing went through her body. Why did this man make her feel the way she did? No one had ever affected her in this way.

"Melanie?"

She was miles away.

When she looked up, Amelie was standing right in front of her. "This is Elena," the child said, holding up a rag doll. "She is my baby, and I have to look after her."

Melanie stared at the doll. "She's very pretty."

Amelie pouted. "No she's not – she's beautiful!"

She scampered away before Melanie could say another word. "She's sweet," she told Philippe. "You are very lucky."

"I am," he replied, but his expression didn't convey his words. "We will talk later. Not while Amelie is around."

He reached over and squeezed her hand. Her insides did all sorts of crazy things. Melanie stared into his eyes.

His eyes that always seemed to read her mind, and see all the way to her soul.

Without warning, the child was back, and sitting on Melanie's knee. Elena, the rag doll, was shoved into her hands. "Can you look after my baby?" she asked, then scampered off again, leaving Melanie bewildered.

"She's full of energy," she blurted out, not meaning to.

"She certainly is," Philippe told her. "She is four. Four-year-olds are full of energy, until they are not. Then they sleep."

"Papa?" Amelie climbed up onto her father's knee. "I am tired, Papa," she said, rubbing both eyes with her little hands.

She had changed into her pajamas, and had a story book in her hand. She pushed the book into her father's hands, then leaned across to Melanie and retrieved her 'baby'.

"You do what you have to do," Melanie told him.

Philippe stood, Amelie holding tight, and began to walk away. "I won't be long," he said.

The sight of father and child was heartwarming. She'd never thought of Philippe as a father, and today's revelation had shook her up.

"Wait!" Amelie shouted. "I must say goodnight to Melanie." Philippe bought her closer, and Amelie wrapped her little arms around Melanie's neck, kissing her on the cheek. "Goodnight Melanie," she said softly, finishing off with a yawn.

"Goodnight, Amelie," she replied softly.

As they left the room, she was surprised at the feelings the tiny human had evoked in her. she had similar feelings for Cody, but he was Sierra and Braxton's baby, and they were related.

This little one was totally unrelated, and they'd only recently met.

She shook herself. She must be going soft, and that would never do.

Besides, she may never see the child again. There were certainly no plans on her part to have further contact.

"That didn't take long." Philippe strolled back into the room. "You should feel privileged – she has never offered Elena to anyone before."

"Never?"

Philippe stared at her, then smiled. "I do not lie to you. Amelie has taken a liking to you, which is not hard to understand."

Melanie decided to change the subject. She wasn't keen on having the child take a shine to her. She wouldn't be around much, and didn't think an attachment would be a good idea.

"You wanted to talk," she said abruptly.

His smile disappeared and was replaced with a frown. She'd said the wrong thing and felt immediately guilty.

"First we eat." He stood and headed for the kitchen. "You stay. I don't make my guests prepare their own food."

He grinned at her and she felt relief. She had clearly upset him, but she had no idea why.

"I'd like to watch the *magnificent Philippe* cook if that's okay?"

"Philippe does not cook – Philippe creates!" he said with a flourish.

She couldn't help herself – a giggle bubbled up from deep inside, and she couldn't stop. Her laughter was apparently contagious because Philippe joined her, and they were both bent over with joy.

Danielle appeared out of nowhere. "What is so funny?" she asked, then waved her hands.

"No, don't tell me, I don't want to know." She smiled, then stared at her brother.

"I'm off now. Amelie is sound asleep," she said. "I am meeting some friends and going to the movies," she told Melanie.

Melanie stepped forward. "It was lovely to meet you," she said, extending her hand. "I hope you have a wonderful evening."

Danielle stepped forward and kissed both her cheeks in the European style. "I am sure we will be meeting again," she said, glancing across to her brother.

And then she was gone.

Philippe began to prepare the food. First he cut potatoes, slicing them carefully and adding them to the oven. He chopped carrots, adding some honey and put them onto cook.

Melanie watched as he cut the chicken into large pieces and covered it with a mixture of garlic, black pepper, herbs and spices, then seared it in a pan. He skillfully cooked the chicken, turning it over as necessary, then threw in some sliced mushrooms.

Last of all he added wine, and let the mixture simmer while he checked the progress of the potatoes.

"Wow, you really are amazing."

Melanie had never witnessed such skill and precision in the kitchen.

"You will get used to it." He winked at her, then returned to his cuisine.

It all looked so...appetizing. "It looks amazing," she said quietly, almost lost for words.

He laughed. "Of course. The great Philippe created it!" He grinned as he went back to the food.

She stared down into the pan. "You make it look so easy. I can barely put a cheese toastie together."

He frowned. "Are you looking after yourself, Melanie?"

"Of course," she said lightheartedly. At least she got a hot meal at work when she wanted one.

Philippe pulled out two dinner plates from a cupboard and placed them on the counter top. He pulled the scalloped potatoes from the oven, and drained the carrots, placing them on the plates as well.

He lifted the pan from the stove and carefully added the chicken mixture to the plates.

Taking each of the plates, he guided Melanie to the table. "Sit, eat, drink," he said, placing a plate in front of her.

"Dare I ask what it is?" She had no clue.

"Madame," he said dramatically. "I present to you Chicken Masala."

Melanie leaned down to breathe it in. "It smells amazing."

Philippe stared at her then chuckled. "It *is* amazing. Philippe created it!"

They both laughed then tucked in.

* * *

After indulging in the incredible melt-in-your-mouth crepes filled with an assortment of fresh berries and topped with strawberry cream, Melanie sat back and patted her belly. "I have never been so blown away by a meal in my entire life." She wiped at her mouth with a linen napkin. How did she know Philippe wouldn't use paper napkins?

A slow smile crossed his lips. "That is because Philippe created it!" They both laughed – it was becoming an private joke between the two of them. One that Melanie was enjoying.

"Seriously though, Melanie," Philippe said quietly. "I am glad you enjoyed it, but I do worry about your eating habits. Perhaps you need to eat here more often." He reached across the table and covered her hand with his own.

She looked down at their entwined hands, and swallowed. Did she dare she risk it? Her heart was already in great peril where this man was concerned.

She swallowed again and stared into his mesmerizing brown eyes. "I could probably endure that incredible hardship," she said seriously.

She meant for it to come across as a joke, but it was no laughing matter.

Was he suggesting they become more than just friends? At this very moment she was so enamored with Philippe, and had no other thoughts on her mind. She wasn't sure if it was the food or the man.

But of course it was the man. She'd felt this way even before she'd come here tonight.

His lopsided grin lit up his face.

She straightened her shoulders. "I recall you wanted to talk?" Her eyes had strayed to his lips and didn't budge. When she finally pulled her gaze away she noticed he was staring at *her* lips.

"What? Do I have food on my mouth?" she asked.

He shook his head. "No, *mon amour*. I was thinking about kissing you, but you're too far away," he said quietly.

What did she say to that? Things were getting too serious, way too quickly.

"Perhaps that is a good thing." Her voice was almost a whisper.

He pushed his chair back and walked the few steps to reach her. "We shall retire to the loungeroom," he said, then put his hand to her back as she stood.

She braced herself for the zing that always ran through her at his touch.

They sat side by side on the couch, the warmth of his knee touching hers was comforting. "I know you have questions," he said, studying her face. "Surely many questions."

He raised his eyebrows.

"*Oui*." She shook her head. She was picking up his habits! "I mean *yes*," she said, shocked that she'd slipped into French so easily and without even thinking.

"That is so cute," he said, grinning. "See, you do remember your high school French." He chuckled, but she didn't think it was amusing at all.

"As you know," he said, taking her by the hand. "Amelie is four. But sadly, she has no mother." He looked to the floor as he caressed her hand.

No mother? How could that be? But she said nothing.

"It is a tragic story," he said quietly. "She was beautiful, Amelie's mother. Inside and out, and we were very much in love." He shook his head sadly.

She squeezed his hand, trying to encourage him.

"We'd been to a family day out. Her family were there, as well as some of my family members. We all got to spend the day together at the zoo. It was an amazing day."

He paused for a moment and swallowed. Melanie could see how difficult this was for him.

"Yvette was eight months pregnant. We were looking forward to the birth of our little one."

He swallowed hard, his jaw tightened, and Melanie could see the distress on his face. All she could do was let him get his story out, and be there to support him.

"We were on our way home, and I was driving." He closed his eyes tight, then flinched as though he'd seen something terrible.

Melanie had a feeling of foreboding. This was not going to end well.

"He came out of nowhere," Philippe said, his eyes still closed tight.

He suddenly opened his eyes wide. "A drunk driver – he drove into the passenger side and killed my beautiful Yvette." His voice was low and shaking and his eyes filled with tears. "The doctors managed to save my Amelie, but her mother was gone."

A tear slid down his face, and Melanie's eyes filled with tears. What could she say? Nothing could make this better.

She leaned in and hugged him, her own face wet with hot tears.

They sat there together, hugging each other tight until Philippe pulled away.

"I'm a terrible host," he said, suddenly standing and wiping at his eyes. He turned and put on some soft music. "Dance with me, Melanie?" he asked softly.

This was a greater risk than any she'd taken before. To be so close to him, to feel his body against hers, it was a torment more than she'd ever endured.

They swayed gently to the music, and Melanie leaned into him, her head resting on his shoulder. She reveled in his gentle touch, and the warmth from his body comforted her.

His lips were close to her ear. "I'm sorry, Melanie," he said gently. "I didn't mean to upset you."

She licked her parched lips. "Please don't apologize."

He reached up, and his hand touched her cheek. "It was hard to say the words, but you had to understand. I couldn't have you hating Amelie's mother for abandoning her."

He pulled back and looked into her face, then placed a finger across her lips. "It is a natural conclusion. I understand."

He pulled his finger away and stared into her eyes. "I'm going to kiss you now," he said gently.

And that's exactly what he did.

Chapter Nine

The lights were low, and Philippe was about to kiss Melanie again.

He was interrupted by his sister rushing through the front door. "I am so sorry; I didn't mean to be so late."

She'd been putting her keys away and finally looked up. "Oh," she said with surprise. "I didn't mean to interrupt."

A sly smile crept across her face. Danielle had been trying to hook him up with other women for far too long. He wasn't ready before – it was hard, very hard – to leave the guilt behind. He would never forget Yvette, but he needed to move on with his life.

Meeting Melanie had been the catalyst. He'd felt something for her almost the moment he'd met her. But she was holding back.

They both were.

"Did you enjoy dinner?" Danielle asked Melanie, who pulled out of his arms to face her. He felt empty without her being so close.

"It was amazing," she answered. "I've never been to a five-star restaurant, but I'm sure that was a five-star meal."

"Only five-star?" He couldn't help himself, and chuckled.

Melanie stared at him. "You are so arrogant," she told him with a grin.

He pulled her close again. "I know, but you love it," he whispered in her ear.

"*Bonne nuit,* goodnight," Danielle said as she left them alone and headed to her room.

"*Bonne nuit,*" Philippe repeated, but was much more interested in the warm body he held close to him.

"Melanie." He said her name slowly, the way she loved him saying it. "Where do we go from here? I...I have feelings for you. Great feelings for you."

She looked up at him. "I have feelings for you too, Philippe. But it's too soon. Perhaps for both of us."

He stared into her face. "You've been hurt too," he said gently. "In a different way."

She told him about Jefferson, about how he'd tried to run her life, even ruin her life. How he'd tried to 'borrow' money from her, and how he had become violent when he didn't get his way.

Luckily her cousin Braxton had been there to protect her.

He caressed her cheek. "You know I will never do anything to harm you, Melanie?" He tipped her chin up and lightly kissed her lips.

When he pulled back, she nodded. "I know. You're not like him." He pulled her into a big bear hug.

"It's late. I should take you home, but I don't want this night to end."

She walked toward the coat stand and snatched up her jacket. "Me either, but we both have to work tomorrow." She said it with regret, and it made his heart race.

As he climbed into the driver's side of his car, his thoughts were of their kiss goodnight when he would leave Melanie at her little unit.

* * *

"Yes Sir," she said confidently. "I will have that rectified immediately."

She disconnected the call and rang housekeeping. "Room ten has *accidentally* smashed a bottle of wine on the wall," she said sighing. "Please send someone up immediately.

I'll send security up as well. I won't put our staff in danger."

Sometimes she wondered if it was really worth the effort of having these celebrity types at the inn, but she knew it was.

The income from VIP's far outweighed the tourist dollars. It was on a close par to the wedding income, but the latter was easier to deal with.

And that reminded her…

She picked up the phone. "Philippe, are you free to finish discussing the wedding garden idea? I promised the bride-to-be I'd get back to her in a couple of weeks, and that time is nearly up."

Since her visit to his house, Melanie had been dodging Philippe. It wasn't that she didn't like him, because she certainly did. It was more that she liked him far too much.

Workplace romances rarely worked. But she knew she was more than smitten, so perhaps keeping her distance was the best option?

She sighed. She didn't want to keep her distance, but she needed to do it for her sanity.

"I'll meet you in the garden," he said with a spring in his voice, and hung up.

Melanie stood and straightened her skirt. She let her hair down, then pulled it back into a tidy bun. She was about to freshen up her lipstick when she realized what she was doing.

"Oh for goodness sakes," she told herself. "This is ridiculous." She stormed out of her office and headed toward the garden.

As she opened the door to the garden area, she saw him standing there, looking all forlorn.

"Melanie," he said in that singsong way he always said her name. She'd missed hearing it the past few days.

She'd managed to avoid him most of the time, but that couldn't continue – they had an upcoming wedding they had to coordinate.

She stood welded to the spot. "Come," he said softly, reaching his hand toward her.

Walking the few steps it took to reach him, her heart pounded. Philippe was no longer just a work colleague, he'd become much more to her.

As she got closer, her hand automatically reached out to his, and he smiled. He'd looked stressed when she first saw him, and wondered if that was her doing.

He squeezed her hand, and his warmth enveloped her, despite them simply standing together.

"This garden, it's quite a mess," he told her. "I think it could work though."

She swallowed. "You do?" Her voice came out a lot quieter than she'd intended.

This would be her first big project for the inn, and she wanted it to be successful.

"Over there," he said pointing to one wall. "That could be where we add the bridal archway."

An archway? That was a great idea. Braxton and Sierra had an archway when they married, and it looked wonderful.

"Chairs here," she said, rushing to where she expected they'd go.

He grinned. "Right. And over there in the far corner, that's where we could have a table for appetizers."

Melanie clapped her hands. "It could work, right?"

He stood staring at her, not saying a word. "Right?" Now she was worried. His eyes never left her face.

He stepped silently toward her, his hand outreached. She stood planted to the spot, her heart thumping in her chest.

He leaned forward, reaching for her hand, then pulled her into a hug, his warmth filling her heart.

"Melanie," he said softly. "I've missed you these past days. Have you changed your mind?" He frowned down at her.

She shook her head. "Just trying to keep it professional."

His fingers hooked under her chin. "Forget professional," he said abruptly. "I'm going to kiss you now."

She leaned into him, relishing the feel of him so close to her. The feeling of being cared for, if not loved, made her feel good. Special.

Their lips touched and Melanie sighed. She felt safe with Philippe, and knew he would never hurt her.

His kiss was gentle, as it always was. She never wanted to leave his side.

She turned away and rested her head against his shoulder. They stood together in silence, her eyes closed, drinking in their precious time together.

Then she reluctantly pulled away.

"So you think this could work?" she asked him in her professional tone, disregarding what had just occurred. What they'd just experienced.

"Melanie…" He shook his head.

"No?" Was he shaking his head because it wouldn't work, or because she'd suddenly turned professional on him?

"*Oui*, it can work," he said on a sigh. "I've made a few notes here for you. Add your own, and speak to Cassie – she has contacts who can do the work. Of course you'll need quotes first."

He passed across the clipboard he'd been scribbling on, and their hands brushed. As much as she'd lied to herself about hoping it didn't happen, she was elated when it did.

"Cassie will require a business plan, so you'll need to get started on that."

She nodded. She had already begun work on her business plan.

"When will I see you again?" he asked quietly.

She studied his face; he looked sad. Did she do that to him?

"I'll call you to organize a meeting for this weekend's wedding."

"*Non*. No. I mean you and me. As a couple, not work." The sadness overtook him again.

She stood in silence considering her options. The thought of not having Philippe in her life was heartbreaking. She couldn't let that happen.

Melanie suddenly felt anticipation at spending quality time with Philippe.

She stared up to the sky. "It's a beautiful day. Perhaps we could have lunch in the park?"

His smile lit up his face. "That would be *magnifique.* I will supply the food."

* * *

Melanie was right, it was a beautiful day. In more ways than one. He'd worried after their evening together that she would pull back. And she had.

Being confronted with a child who wasn't your own, and the truth about the child's mother, was enough to send any woman running.

But Melanie was tough. He'd known that from the moment he met her. The first time.

He'd liked her that first time too. Not that he'd spent a lot of time with her then. He was preparing the wedding reception, and she was Sierra's bridesmaid. They were both busy.

Even on that incredibly hectic day, he'd felt the connection.

When she'd walked into his kitchen on her first day on the job, a thrill went through him. And to find out she would be working with him, coordinating on the events, that was even better.

Right now he needed to concentrate on what he was doing – packing a picnic lunch. Melanie had agreed to go to the park with him.

No. *Melanie had suggested they go to the park.* That was even better. His heart was soaring, and he felt it beating in his chest.

He wandered around the kitchen choosing items for his picnic basket.

The inn had a number of baskets on hand, as guests often ordered a filled picnic basket for their day trips.

"Do you want me to do that, Chef?" Adam asked. "I didn't know we'd had an order or I would have done it by now."

"Thank you, but no, Adam. I've got this." He glanced up at Adam, a grin on his face.

"You've got another hot date."

"Perhaps."

Adam cleared his throat. "It's with that cute chicki-babe Melanie. Am I right?"

Philippe stood to his full height, towering over Adam. "Do not disrespect Melanie. Do you understand," he said, pushing a finger into Adam's chest.

Adam's hands shot up and he stepped back. "Whoa. I was just stirring you up, Chef. I promise."

"That's alright then." He continued on his quest choosing items for his picnic basket.

When he was done, he grabbed some cans of soda, adding them to the basket, and was on his way.

Melanie was waiting out the front of the inn, lapping up the sun.

Philippe leaned in and stole a kiss on her cheek when he arrived. A little cheeky, he knew, but after their dinner...perhaps he'd get away with it.

Melanie turned and smiled at him. "Ready?" she asked, then reached down and took his hand.

Philippe was not going to complain. "Danielle is at the park with Amelie this afternoon. Do you mind?"

She didn't even think about it. "Of course not. She's a delight, that daughter of yours."

His relief was palpable. He was worried Melanie might see Amelie more of a nuisance than anything. After all, she was not used to children. Sierra and Braxton's baby Cody was only a few months old, so he didn't count.

Melanie seemed relaxed, which made him happy. She was definitely stressed earlier, when they'd met in the garden.

As they approached the park, he saw Amelie in the distance. Danielle grabbed her hand as she threatened to run off. She was rather prone to doing that.

"She's so sweet," Melanie told him. "She wants to see her Papa."

"Her Papa wants to see her too. I miss her when I'm at work."

She squeezed his hand. "I'm sure she misses you too."

As they approached the park bench, two little arms wrapped around his legs. "Papa," she said, hugging his legs tight.

He reached down and pulled her into his arms. "Amelie," he said, feeling elated to have both his girls with him at that very moment.

* * *

The final wedding reception for the month of May was well underway.

A wedding *she* had arranged. Her first successful wedding. Her heart sang.

Melanie stood looking around the room, trying to gauge if everything was running smoothly. Fingers crossed, so far everything was going fine.

The bride sat at the bridal table, resplendent in her stunning gown, the handsome groom beside her. They had their heads together, quietly talking despite all the noise going on around them.

Ah, true love.

Philippe had been in the kitchen most of the day, making sure everything was going to plan. He would be shouting orders to the kitchen staff, and ensuring everything was running smoothly.

It was nearly time for the desserts to be served, so the pressure was mostly off. Another half an hour, and they would all breathe a sigh of relief.

The reception would still be ongoing, but it would be at the tail end – just a few more speeches, and some music to finish off with.

She looked up as she heard banging on the bridal table.

The Best Man stood, champagne in hand and waited for the noise to die down. "To the Bride and Groom – John and Penelope. May they have a long and happy marriage."

The guests responded. "To the Bride and Groom."

Glasses clinked all around the room.

The Best Man sat down again, and the mumbling started up once again.

Right on time, Philippe appeared at the kitchen doorway. He stepped aside for the servers to deliver the desserts to the guests.

Melanie began to wander around ensuring all the guests were happy. Philippe did the same, chatting to a number of guests along the way. He was so much better at this than she was.

"They look delicious," she said quietly as he came to stand beside her.

"We shall sample them later, *mon amour*," he whispered.

She chuckled. Philippe always ensured there were plenty of leftovers, and she wasn't complaining.

Crackers and cheese, and dinner mints were delivered to each table, along with tea and coffee.

Ten minutes later, the band began to play again, and a few couples moved out onto the dance floor.

Philippe grabbed her by the hand. "Shall we?"

She frowned. "We can't gatecrash someone's wedding."

"Pfffft. They won't mind." He coerced her onto the dance floor, then pulled her close. The music was gentle, and together they swayed to the music.

Melanie closed her eyes and rested her head on Philippe's shoulder, and everything else disappeared. Her heart fluttered; she knew she was falling more for this man every time she saw him. Did he feel the same about her?

"Melanie," he said in his familiar singsong way. "I am falling hard for you."

She looked up at him, dismayed at his words. Was she ready for commitment? She wasn't sure.

He took advantage of her confusion and covered her lips with his own. His kiss was gentle, and she felt his hand go up her back and to her hair.

He dismantled her bun and slid his fingers through her long silky hair.

She was lost to the world.

Until she heard applause.

She turned around to see all the guests clapping. The servers and kitchen staff were lined up outside the kitchen and were all grinning. They too were clapping.

"Philippe," she spat. "Look what you have done."

She tried to pull away, but he enveloped her, and pulled her closer still. "Ignore them," he said, then leaned down and kissed her again.

Chapter Ten

It was Sunday, and they'd decided to go to the zoo. It was a long drive from their little outback town, but it would be worth it.

But it would be difficult for Philippe, considering what had happened after his last trip to a zoo.

He'd told her Amelie was excited, as she'd never been before, and she'd never seen wild animals, except in books and on the television.

She heard Philippe's car pull up, and went to open the door, her heart pounding in anticipation.

He guided Amelie into the unit for the first time ever. Melanie watched with amusement as Amelie looked around. "You have a *very* small house," she said bluntly.

"Amelie…" Philippe warned, his tone stern.

"It's okay," Melanie told him. "She's used to your big farmhouse."

She went and stood next to the child, crouching down to her height. "I live here by myself, Amelie," she said quietly. "So I don't need much space."

Amelie stared at her. "You could come and live with us. Papa wouldn't mind, would you, Papa?"

Melanie was at first aghast, then realized as a child, Amelie would not understand the implications.

Philippe grinned, and opened his mouth to speak, but changed his mind. Instead he changed the subject. "Are we ready to go?"

"Yes! I want to see the elephants, and the tigers, and the seals, and the…"

Her father laughed. "You want to see everything. Time to go, little one."

They piled into the car and were soon on their way.

As they stood outside the huge gates to the zoo, Amelie looked up and stared, her eyes opened wide. "It's as big as the whole world," she said loudly.

Melanie laughed and heard laughter around them. "Wait until you see how big the elephants are."

"Are they *this* big?" Amelie spread her arms wide.

"Not even close. Come," Philippe said, lifting her up onto his shoulders.

As they walked through the massive gates, Melanie squeezed his hand. She knew today was going to be incredibly difficult for Philippe as he would likely recall the worst day of his life.

When they were close to the elephant enclosure, he put Amelie to the ground, and she ran ahead of them. "Papa, papa! Look at the elephants!" Her eyes were wide with awe.

He squeezed her hand.

"See the Mama with the baby elephant," Philippe pointed out.

Her eyes opened wide in amazement. "Look, Melanie. There's a baby!" Amelie stretched out her little arm and pointed.

It almost felt like they were a family.

* * *

The business plan was written and approved. The budget set and money allocated.

They'd decided to make a glass roof on the garden, to make it an all-weather wedding garden. Melanie was more than excited, she was overjoyed about her very own wedding project.

Philippe had provided a lot of input, since this project was going to affect him and his team, but overall it was her baby.

She left her office and went outside to what she'd dubbed the *wedding garden*. They already had a number of bookings for the new wedding package, and it wasn't even finished yet.

The area was about half the size of the reception hall, and Melanie had no idea why it had been neglected for so long.

"It's looking wonderful, Jimmy," she told the contractor doing the work.

He was bent over, digging holes to anchor the archway. He stood up to talk with her. "You won't know the place when it's finished," he said. "Once the concreting is done, and the flooring is down, the gardeners will come in and work their magic."

"I can't wait." She could see it now – the first wedding would be such a celebration. And a real achievement for not only her, but also the Oakdale Inn. "I'll leave you to it," she said, and returned to her office.

The best thing that had ever happened to her was to accept Sierra and Braxton's offer to work here. Not only had it relieved her stress, it had changed her life in many ways.

The month of May had been life-changing. Melanie didn't think she would ever be able to say that, but it was true. Not only did she have an amazing job, one that bought a sense of achievement each and every day, but she had met her soulmate.

She brought her hands to her heart. Her eyes sparkled with unshed tears at the sheer joy she felt.

* * *

Melanie waited outside the main entrance of the inn.

It was becoming a habit to have lunch in the park with Philippe on the sunny days. One that she loved.

She lifted her face to the sky, eyes closed, basking in the sunshine.

She felt a gentle kiss on her cheek and opened her eyes abruptly. "Philippe! You scared me," she said, breathless.

"Apologies, *mon amour,*" he said with regret in his voice. "I didn't mean to scare you. Quite the opposite." He reached down and wrapped his fingers around hers.

She spotted the picnic basket in his other hand and smiled.

"You know, you don't have to always provide lunch. I can do my bit too."

"Ah, but mine is more tasty," he said arrogantly, then grinned. He liked to stir her up, and she knew it.

"Says who?" she said cheekily, then began to pull him along the path toward the park. She looked back over her shoulder in time to see his lopsided grin.

She'd tried keeping her distance and it really hadn't worked, so had decided just to give in. After all, she really did like Philippe, and he'd told her liked her too. A lot.

They arrived at the park and took up residence in the park bench they sat on most times they came here. She liked it there because they could see right across the park. The view was glorious.

They sat close together, and her leg rubbed up against his. She didn't mind one bit, and was sure Philippe felt the same.

"You make the yummiest food," she said between bites. "Much better than the ham and cheese sandwiches I bring from home."

He frowned at her. "Why are you not ordering a nice lunch at work?"

She fidgeted on the park bench. "I feel bad ordering a hot meal every day." She squirmed a little more.

"Melanie," he said quietly. "It is a perk of the job. Our bosses, your cousins, want to look after us." He pulled a mini quiche out of the basket. "See this? These were made this morning. They were on the lunch menu today, along with a crispy salad.

He threw his hands up in the air. "And you want ham and cheese sandwiches!"

She pulled a face at him.

"Very mature," he said, laughing. He reached for her hand, and enveloped it in his own. "This is what I love about you, Melanie," he said suddenly serious and gazing into her eyes. "You are smart, fun to be around, and you are perfect."

He kissed the back of her hand, then brought it up to his cheek. "You, Melanie Chalmers, are very special to me."

Suddenly all the birds and ducks from the pond went flying up into the air, squawking as they did so.

Melanie glanced up and saw a small figure running toward them.

"Papa! Melanie!"

Little legs ran as fast as they could go.

"Amelie!" Philippe stood, releasing Melanie's hand as he did so. She suddenly felt empty, bereft. Why did Philippe make her feel the way he did?

He opened his arms to his daughter, reaching out in readiness to hug her. She could watch him interact with Amelie all day.

Reaching down, he picked the child up and hugged her tightly. "Where is aunt Danielle?" he asked, looking across the park.

"She's coming, she's just very slow," Amelie said with a pout.

"Tsk, Amelie. That is not nice."

She buried her head into her father's shoulder. Philippe was strict with Amelie, but also loved her very much.

"Did you say hello to Melanie." Amelie lifted her head and looked sideways at her, then a grin spread across her face.

"Hello Amelie," Melanie said, happy to see the child again.

"*Bonjour*, Melanie," she said excitedly, then quickly buried her head again.

"Ah, here comes aunt Danielle now."

"What are you doing here, Papa?" Amelie stared into her father's face, and touched his chin with her fingers. "Yuck, you need a shave. You're all bristly."

Philippe laughed and put his daughter to the ground. Melanie laughed with him. She was such a sweet child, but she came out with the funniest things at times.

Melanie reached across and ran her own fingers across his cheek and chin. "You are right, Amelie," she said. "He is all bristly." She couldn't help but grin.

Philippe caught her hand in his own. "You are in dangerous territory," he whispered, so only she could hear.

She licked her lips. He was right – it *was* dangerous. Just touching him stirred up feelings in her. Feelings she'd never felt with anyone else before.

The sort of feelings that left her wanting more. Wanting him more. They stared into each other's eyes. It was like a silent pact. One that said I know what you're thinking because I'm thinking it too.

He leaned in and kissed her gently. On the lips. In front of his daughter!

"Yeeew, Papa! That is gross."

He moved away and glanced down. "No it's not, little one. Adults kiss each other when they are in love."

In love? Was he saying he loved her? Her heart fluttered in her chest.

He turned his head and stared at her, daring her to disagree.

"Do you love Melanie, Papa?" Her little head titled up to look at her Papa.

His eyes never left Melanie's face. "Yes, little one, I do love Melanie. Very much."

She reached for Melanie's hand and pulled on it. "Do you love my Papa?" Her eyes were open wide in anticipation.

Melanie's heart began to pound. She felt light-headed, but she also felt ecstatic. She looked down at the sweet little girl pulling on her hand. "You know, I think I just might," she said quietly.

Philippe pulled her close. "My sweet Melanie, I love you more than words can say." He reached into his pocket and pulled out a small box, popping it open."

Melanie stared at him, then at the ring he held out to her. "Will you marry me, Melanie?" He slid down onto one knee, and gazed up at her lovingly.

She was in love with this man, had been almost from the moment they'd met. Sure he could be infuriating sometimes, and he was definitely arrogant, especially when it came to his cooking. But other times he was so loving and special.

Despite all that, she backed off. Her hands went to her heart and she stared at him. "You want me to marry you? Is this a joke?"

He looked hurt. "It isn't a joke." He closed the ring box and sat down on the park bench. "Do you not love me, *mon amour*?"

Her heart did a little flip-flop. "Oh, but I do. I love you very much. It's just…"

Amelie pulled on the hem of her skirt. "Are you going to be my Mama?" Wide open eyes stared up at her.

In that moment, Melanie's heart almost broke. Her eyes filled with tears. How could she say no to this man? The man she'd grown to love over such a short time. And the little girl who had won over her heart, bit by bit?

He stepped forward and pulled her into a hug. "Don't say yes unless you mean it," he said softly.

"Yes," she said quietly. He pulled back and stared at her. "Yes," she said, more loudly this time.

Philippe picked her up and spun her about.

"Papa, what are you doing?" Amelie laughed as she watched her papa go a little crazy.

"Melanie said yes. She is going to be your Mama!" He put Melanie back on her feet, and Amelie wrapped her little arms around Melanie's legs.

"What's going on here," Danielle asked as she finally caught up to them.

"She said yes," Philippe told his sister.

"And about time too," Danielle said firmly.

Chapter Eleven

Melanie stood quietly in the doorway to the Wedding Garden, Sierra Chalmers at her side.

She looked about, taking in all the elements of this beautiful area. There were garden beds on three sides of the area, overflowing with seasonal flowers and foliage, almost a showcase for the area. The was a large serviceable table in the back corner, where the kitchen staff would place trays of food to be distributed before the guests moved into the reception hall. Pre-dinner drinks would also be served from here.

Behind the table a large cupboard had been built – this would store the chairs when they weren't in use.

But the thing that really stood out to Melanie was the bridal archway. The very one that Sierra and Braxton had stood beneath for their wedding.

When Sierra found out what Melanie was planning, she insisted they use her archway. After all, it was sitting unused in one of the inn's storage units. It might as well go to good use, she had said.

And it would certainly do that.

Melanie never dreamed, when she embarked on the Wedding Garden project, that she and Philippe would be the first couple to be married there.

Philippe turned from where he stood beside the archway and looked back at her, Braxton at his side. His face lit up, and she knew that was for her. Only for her.

The music began, and she leaned down, encouraging Amelie to walk forward and throw the rose petals to either side of her.

A excited thrill went down her spine. She turned to Sierra. "Thank you," she whispered.

Sierra looked puzzled. "For what?"

"For giving me this job, for helping me meet my soulmate." Her eyes filled with tears, but Melanie was determined not to let them flow for fear of ruining her makeup.

Sierra leaned in and hugged her. "Always happy to help."

Melanie watched as the other woman also blinked back tears. They were a fine pair.

"Hurry up, Melanie," Amelie shouted from the archway where she stood with her Papa. "It's time for you to be my Mama."

Everyone laughed but that didn't deter Amelie. She stood with a pout on her face, and her hands on her hips. Philippe leaned in and whispered something to her, and Amelie dropped the basket, then ran back to her, her little arms outstretched.

When she arrived, Amelie took Melanie's hand. "Come with me," she said confidently. "I will show you the way."

And that's exactly what she did.

* * *

It was difficult for Philippe to keep his place at the bridal table. He kept stealing glances toward the kitchen.

"They'll be fine," Melanie whispered in his ear. "Do you honestly think your staff would dare to let down the great Philippe?"

She grinned and he chuckled.

"No, *mon amour*," he said. "They wouldn't dare."

Braxton stood up to make his speech as Best Man. Melanie groaned.

"I've known Melanie since we were small – we are cousins after all. There are so many stories I could tell you, most of them pretty darned juicy. She used to get up to a lot of *questionable* stuff, but I think Mel would never forgive me."

There was a collective groan around the room. "So instead, I'll ask you to raise your glasses and toast the bride and groom."

Melanie breathed a sigh of relief as everyone raised their glasses. "To Melanie and Philippe."

The music began and Braxton introduced the bridal waltz.

The new bride and groom and got up from their seats and headed for the dance floor, Melanie in her beautiful wedding dress, and Philippe in his smart white suit.

They stood close together and the music began. "I can't believe we're married, *mon amour*," Philippe whispered in her ear.

"Same," she said. "It seems like a dream. I keep wondering if this is real."

They floated around the room, moving to the rhythm of the music, and Melanie rested her head on Philippe's shoulder.

Until she felt tugging on her dress. When she looked down, Amelie stood there, her hands on her hips. "When do I get to dance with Papa?" she asked innocently.

Philippe reached down and scooped her up. "Right now, little one. You can dance with Papa and Mama."

Melanie's eyes filled with tears. They were finally a family.

Epilogue

*O*ne Year Later...

"Papa, Papa! Come quick!" Amelie called to her father who was fixing lunch.

Philippe dropped what he was doing and ran to her. The urgency in her voice told him something was very wrong.

"It's Mama," she said as she ran into the kitchen. "She's wet herself," she whispered conspiratorially. "And now she's laying on the floor in the loungeroom holding her tummy."

He ran to his wife. "What can I do," he asked, panicked at the thought their baby was on the way.

Melanie winced as she smiled up at him. "It's time," she said as she winced again.

"I'll call Danielle first. She'll need to collect Amelie."

He was running around collecting up her suitcase and other necessities for the hospital. "Philippe," she said abruptly. "There's no time. Get me to the hospital now or you will be delivering this baby."

"Surely you jest," he said.

"Do I look like I'm joking? Get me to the damned hospital," she said between clenched teeth.

Amelie started to cry. "What's wrong with Mama?" She leaned in and hugged her precious Mama. "Papa, what's wrong with Mama?"

"It's time for your little baby brother or sister to arrive," Melanie said gently. "No need to cry." She hugged Amelie tight and rubbed her hands over the child's back to comfort her.

Amelie pulled back and looked into her face, her eyes wide. "Really? Our new baby is coming today?"

Without another word, Philippe scooped her up and carried her out to the car. "Amelie, come now. Aunt Danielle will collect you from the hospital."

Without another word, Amelie ran to the car and climbed into her booster seat, and they were soon on their way.

* * *

Danielle met them at the emergency department.

Philippe had called ahead and they were waiting for Melanie's arrival. They were taken to a birthing suite immediately.

"Mama, Papa!" Amelie called urgently as they were whisked away.

"Be good for aunt Danielle," Philippe told her gently. "Soon you will see the new baby."

Her little eyes lit up, and she hugged her Papa tightly.

Danielle had to hold her back. It broke his heart, but he had to stay with Melanie. Wanted to stay with Melanie.

Philippe sat on the side of the bed holding Melanie's hand, where he'd sat for the past couple of hours, despite a chair being beside the bed.

He leaned in and kissed Melanie on the cheek. "I love you very much, *mon amour*," he whispered.

"I love you too," she said, her expression questioning.

"I just wanted to hear you say that before you become murderous," he said, chuckling and moving away as she tried to punch his arm.

A midwife came in and checked her over. "Okay, Melanie," she said. "It's all happening now. I'll go and get the doctor. Philippe will be right here with you."

His heart thudded. Their baby was about to arrive.

* * *

"Shhh, quietly now."

Philippe carried Amelie into Melanie's hospital room. "Baby Gabriel is asleep. Be very quiet and don't wake him up."

Amelie put her fingers to her lips, her eyes wide with excitement.

She put her arms out to hug Melanie, so Philippe took her closer. Amelie kissed her on the cheek, then he took her closer to the baby.

He was wrapped tightly in a blanket and sound asleep, his little fingers peeking out the top. Philippe leaned over so she could see him better.

"Oh!" she said with excitement. "Look at his tiny fingers!"

"He is tiny," Philippe said. "And you are his big sister."

"Oooh," she said quietly. "I am Gabriel's big sister?"

She closed her eyes and began to cry. "That is wonderful, Papa," she said between tears.

Melanie reached out to her husband and daughter. "We have our own little family," she said between her own tears.

Melanie said a silent prayer of thanks to Sierra and Braxton who set this all in motion.

<u>The End</u>

Thank you so much for reading my book – I hope you enjoyed it.

I would greatly appreciate you leaving a review on Amazon, even if it is only a one-liner. It helps to have my books more visible on Amazon!

If you haven't already, you might like to read about Melanie's cousin, Braxton. His story can be found here.

All my books can be seen on my [Amazon Author Page.](#)

www.ingramcontent.com/pod-product-compliance
Lightning Source LLC
Chambersburg PA
CBHW071531100726
47908CB00004B/1359